JAHEEWAH

God Of The Winds

JOHN ARNN

ArnnWorks Publishing

NASHVILLE, TN

Acknowledgements...

The idea for *Jaheewah* happened over forty years ago. In all those years, there were hundreds of conversations with friends and colleagues, too many to name, who provided insightful comments, professional expertise, and encouragement. This book would not be what it is without those conversations. To those who shared with me their knowledge, expertise, and encouragement, I offer my sincere gratitude.

Probably the most constant and heart-warming support and patience in this project was provided by my wife, Sally Mae, whose many discussions with me were invaluable.

I was fortunate to have the assistance of an incredible editor, Heather Webber, who had the good grace to only smile and not laugh out loud when I told her that I didn't think she would find very much to edit. She not only did the mundane chore of correcting comma usage and syntax, she played a vital part in clarifying elements of research that were sometimes problematic, particularly with medical information.

Finally, I wish to thank Peter Rosenberger who has kindly become my mentor for laboring through all of the issues related to publication. I was his mentor some thirty years ago when he was my student at Belmont University. So we have come full circle. It is through Peter I met Thom King of King Author Productions, who did the book design and formatting. I am grateful for his talents. Thanks also to Jenna Dawn Arsenault and Matthew Arnn for their cover art work.

Thanks one and all.

John Arnn

For

Sally Mae
Benjamin and Matthew
Jenna Dawn and Carter

The sun had risen in a cloudless sky heating the marshes and the tide-drained sandy beds which led to the tidal river. Invisible to the naked eye, rising hot air currents pushed against the underside of his long and narrow outstretched wings. He caught the elusive lift and rode it all the way up and out of the doughnut-shaped thermal. Looking toward the river far below, he began his descent and entry into another thermal, methodically working his way toward the deeper estuaries.

He soared fifty feet above the smooth surface when the flash of silver just below triggered his hunting instinct. He quickly turned out of the rising air current, watched his prey intently, and increased the angle of glide. Descending rapidly, he slowly opened his hooked beak and stretched the powerful leg tendons—

readying the deadly talons for the kill. It would not be easy—the timing must be perfect. For a while he would fly the same line as the fish—watching his every movement, anticipating the thrust that would propel the fish out of the water. It happened quickly—almost beautifully. A slight turn of the powerful wings and he was on it, his razor-sharp talons snatching the fish from the natural safety of deeper water. Sharp spicules on the soles of his fleshy toes held the slippery victim until needle-taloned feet drew the life from it. With forceful downstrokes of his wings, the magnificent bird sought higher and safer air and the invisible path to his island nest.

6:49 a.m. Perry Station, Hagers Point, South Carolina. 1972.

"Name?"

"Robert Hendrick . . . with the Charleston *Courier*."

Dressed in denim trousers, sport shirt and tan windbreaker, Hendrick could easily have passed for one of the young research personnel of the island's marine biology institute. His thick and curly brown hair made him appear taller than his five feet eleven inches. His tanned face revealed a pleasant seriousness and sensitivity reflected in others whom he respected—his editor, a pilot friend, the teacher of Learning Disability Students he recently interviewed.

"Boarding pass, please!" The captain of the ferry, recognizing Hendrick as an "outsider," gently reminded him of the departure schedule. Hendrick reached into his jacket pocket and produced the pre-arranged pass given to him by his editor who had set up Hendrick's visit to the island. Though mainly a formality now, a visit to the Institute still required special permission. He found the island's cloistered nature intriguing and looked forward to the experience.

"We've been waiting our five minute limit for you, Mr. Hendrick. You almost missed the run. Come on aboard."

"Well, you see, it took a little time to get a taxi to bring me . . ."

"Shove off!" yelled the old man to the deck hand.

"Mr. Hendrick, there's nothing I'd rather do than hear about your difficulty in getting here, but most of these people have been getting to Jaheewah on time for twenty-seven years, and they kind of expect today to be no different. So, if you'll excuse me?"

"Sure. Sorry I held you up." *Crusty old coot*, he thought to himself. Hendrick stepped into the enclosed cabin area and sat near a window, putting his suitcase, portable typewriter, and camera on the seat beside him. Amused at the occasional glances from the "regulars," he began to study the passengers, wondering what kind of work each did on the island. Here sat several maintenance men, identified by the logo on their shirts. Up front a few seats, two bearded men, considerably younger than their fellow passengers, were engrossed in conversation, frequently gesturing with their hands and pointing toward the southern part of the island—scientists, obviously. Above the roar of the diesel engines, bits of their conversation indicated a friendly argument was in progress—about crustaceans or the frustrating sex life of the North American crab, Hendrick supposed.

Abruptly, the engines were shut down—much too soon, Hendrick thought, to be arriving at the island dock. Most of the passengers seemed equally surprised and looked up from their newspapers to see that a small sailboat had crossed in front of the larger vessel. The old captain slid the port side window open and yelled something at two young boys in a small craft. The larger of the boys responded by giving the captain the finger. Then, trimming the sails, he eased his boat out of the ferry's path.

During this interruption in the trip, nearly everyone's attention focused on the exchange between the captain and the two boys. Hendrick realized that the two scientist types were oblivious to the confrontation and that their conversation was more intense. He heard them plainly now.

"I'm telling you—I was there when they found him, and it just doesn't make sense," said the heavier of the two. At that moment, the engines revved up, and their conversation was lost in the diesel's roar and the hissing spray against the hull.

JAHEEWAH

Hendrick continued to watch the two men. They had ended their conversation when one of them glanced toward the rear of the cabin. Noticing Hendrick, he turned back to his colleague and muttered something. The other briefly took note of Hendrick and then turned forward again. Hendrick wondered if they had just then realized who he was. Both appeared to Hendrick a little apprehensive about his presence. He remembered his editor's last instructions. *"We're giving you space for five separate articles about the Institute. I think they are doing good work and really need a PR boost. So, see if you can help with that. They will be expecting you, but don't expect a lot of VIP treatment. Oh, and here's a story from the wire service you should probably read and look into before you get down there.* Oddly enough, Hendrick had thought of touring the Marine Biology Institute on Jaheewah Island as a pleasant diversion rather than a covert investigation on the story the editor had given him. But now—now, this strange premonition of intrigue about the island and the people on it captured his attention.

The story from his editor seemed rather cut and dried. A noted marine biologist fails to return from a specimen gathering expedition and a day later floats into shore.

Hendrick gazed blankly forward as he considered the possible significance of the earlier comment from the man in the front of the cabin: *". . . it doesn't make sense."* He then realized that a passenger had turned and was speaking to him.

"I'm sorry," Hendrick answered, "I couldn't hear you."

The man held out his newspaper. "I said, it'll be another fifteen minutes before we dock. Would you like to read this week's paper?"

Hendrick took the paper and replied, "Yes, I would. Thanks."

Looking at the small local weekly, Hendrick remembered his last days at the school of journalism. His best friends, upon graduation, had landed jobs with large metropolitan newspapers. They couldn't understand why he didn't want that kind of success. Hendrick was often amused at the thought of these young, inexperienced cub reporters nosing around city halls and senate chambers for the slightest smell of graft or conspiracy. What Hendrick really wanted was editorial control over a smaller daily or bi-weekly—like the one in his hands. He instinctively began to categorize all of the improvements needed to clean up the front page. *"Look at this,"* he thought to himself. *"Too many sentences in the lead paragraph."* A left-hand column article about the work of the City Council reported that the mayor was recuperating from the surgical removal of a large growth. Adjacent to this paragraph was a three-column picture of produce farmer Lucas Harrison delicately holding a fifteen-pound cucumber. Hendrick broke up thinking of the possible locations of the mayor's growth.

As Hendrick turned the page, his eyes were drawn to a headline in the top left column.

NOTED MARINE BIOLOGIST
ACCIDENTALLY DROWNS
HAGERS POINT, SOUTH CAROLINA.

Dr. Heinrich Eduard Stassen, world famous authority on invertebrates and small fishes, accidentally drowned last week while tending a research project on the southern tip of Jaheewah Island. Dr. Thomas Farrow, founder and Head of Jaheewah Island Marine Biology Research Institute, spoke of Dr. Stassen's death as ". . . an immeasurable loss—not only to the Institute but to the entire world as well. Stassen's work on epidemic diseases in invertebrates is of inestimable value in toxins prevention. His residency gave us almost immediate world recognition and helped us attract the finest students in every field of marine biology. We can—we would never have been able to repay him for his influence and direction. We all regret Dr. Stassen's unfortunate death more than anyone will ever know." A memorial service for Dr. Stassen has been planned for Wednesday at 2:00 p.m. in the Cha-

pel of Jaheewah Presbyterian Church. His remains are to be cremated and the ashes scattered at sea following the memorial service. Dr. Stassen had no known living relatives. On Wednesday, all activities of the Institute have been cancelled in Dr. Stassen's honor.

Hendrick looked up from the paper and glanced out the window. As the shoreline of the inland river slid past him, he watched the graceful but deadly dives of waterfowl yanking fish from their presumably safe world. Hendrick realized he had just witnessed a link in the ecological chain but thought to himself, *"The poor slobs never know what hits them."* A line from a poem or something he had recently read formed in his mind: *"Fate, O most dispassionate and eternal of masters."*

As he pondered the origin of this thought, he drifted into philosophical daydreaming about life and its all too frequent unfairness. He recalled his recent story on Joseph and Carrie Swatzer. They had spent nearly thirty years in their tiny corner drugstore.

10

Shot in a hold-up two years past and now paralyzed, Joseph Swatzer could only offer customers a smile or a joke, while Carrie ran the business. The assailant spent two hours in jail. The brutal attack happened too quickly for them to understand. Their lease came up for renewal, but the building was sold, and the new owner, a conglomerate, planned complete razing of the building for a shopping mall. The Swatzers had no family, no funds to relocate, and no will to struggle. They decided to retire—literally—and were found dead in each other's arms in their small apartment. Their heads nearly above water, they too were snatched and devoured by progress.

Diesel fumes had begun to nauseate Hendrick, and he sighed in relief as the engines slowed and the pitch of the boat leveled. The passengers gathered their belongings and moved aft to disembark. Hendrick decided to wait until the aisle cleared before picking up his suitcase and typewriter. He nodded politely to most of the passengers but carefully noted the facial expressions of the two scientists as they passed. They seemed to regard him as foreign and unwelcome. He could not resist testing this hostile environment.

"Are you gentlemen with the Institute?"

"Yes, we are," the larger man replied with a slight German accent.

Extending his hand, Hendrick introduced himself. "Robert Hendrick with the *Courier*. I'm doing several articles on the Institute, and I'd like to talk with you both sometime."

The scientist answered, "Well, Mr. Hendrick, we were told you were coming and asked to be available to you, but you must realize that we are all quite busy." Half smiling, he continued, "I hope you will not take offense if we all do not line up to chat with you. I'm sure we will, in time, have an opportunity to answer any of your questions. Excuse us, please?"

"I . . . uh, didn't get your names."

"Frederick Gruber and this is Jack Morrison. I am very sorry. We have to go now."

"Sure. I'll see you again, I imagine."

The two men intrigued Hendrick with their obvious apprehension about his presence. He felt certain that further conversation would be at his insistence.

The boat had been moored, and the aisle had cleared, so Hendrick left the cabin and stepped up onto the deck. The bright sun made him squint momentarily as he scanned the dock for whomever was to meet him. It was a small dock with a wood-framed enclosure, a few benches along a weathered fence, and immediately behind them, a few parked cars. The sunlight reflected painfully off the windows.

Soon, only the dock crew and a few men fishing remained. Hendrick glanced at two small runabouts tied up at the edge of the dock. Both had the initials JIMBRI painted on them. "Jaheewah Island Marine Biology Research Institute," he said aloud. He also noticed a small passenger van with the same logo painted on the sides. The driver of the van placed some cartons in the back, then drove away. Only a vintage WWII jeep remained in the parking area. Hendrick casually looked around and muttered to himself, "*I didn't really expect a marching band, but this is ridiculous.*" Hendrick surveyed the parking area, and as he waited, the quietness and solitude of the island and the pleasant warmth began to affect him. Seeing no one else, he took a seat on one of the benches placed there for waiting passengers. After a few seconds, a blast of the jeep's horn immediately behind the fence railing nearly catapulted him back onto the deck of the boat twenty yards away. Hendrick turned to see a middle-aged man slouched behind the wheel with, Hendrick thought, the slightest trace of a devious smile on his face.

He walked to the driver's side, tempted to jerk the old man out of the jeep and punch him in the mouth.

The driver took a look at Hendrick and his gear and said, "You Hendricks?"

"That's right—Hendrick," he snapped, emphasizing the singular.

"Figured so, since you was the only one left. My name's Jason. Get in."

Jason spoke with a slow, heavy southern accent that took Hendrick a few minutes to get accustomed to. The more they talked, the easier it was to understand everything Jason had to say, and Hendrick found his manner of speech both attractive and expressive.

Hendrick tossed his suitcase and typewriter in the back of the vehicle, keeping his trusty Minolta SR-T 101 over his shoulder, and went around to the passenger side. He slammed the door and said, "I didn't see you sitting here—the sun reflecting on the glass. I guess it was too much trouble for you to just call my name instead of scaring the crap out of me."

"Didn't mean to scare you, Mr. Hendricks," he drawled. "Just wanted to let you know I was here waitin' on you." He looked at Hendrick and smiled broadly. "The H.I. said I was to meet you an' take you around the island."

"H.I.?" repeated Hendrick.

"Farrow . . . Head of the Institute," Jason replied. "He thought you might like to see a little of the island, an' he couldn't get away hisself to meet you. So . . . you got yourself a tour unless you got other plans."

Hendrick eyed his thin and deeply tanned companion curiously. Except for the little game he played with him at the dock, Jason seemed a likable old cuss. Hendrick would learn that Jason was an administrator's dream. He knew every inch of the island, knew every piece of equipment well enough to rebuild it, and was steadfastly loyal. Farrow trusted Jason implicitly with the maintenance crew. His trust was well-placed for Jason seldom presented the H.I. with personnel problems. Hendrick also discovered that Jason's perception and sensitivity were on a par with any well-trained psychologist. Very few employees knew that they had Jason to thank for their jobs, or conversely, to blame for their dismissal.

Hendrick grinned at him and said, "Okay, Mr. Tour Director, lead the way."

Jason rammed the jeep in gear and sped down the narrow paved lane leading away from the dock. The road was full of potholes which drew in the tires like magnets. It wasn't that Jason tried to hit all of them—

he just didn't try to miss any. About a half-mile later, the road dead-ended at a T-junction, and Jason brought the jeep to a quick halt.

Hendrick asked, "Where did you get this jeep?"

"The H.I. got a good deal from Army Surplus an' bought three of 'em. We figured if we had three, we ought to be able to keep one runnin' pretty good."

A calm settled over the vehicle that startled Hendrick in its quietness. Hendrick looked behind him to see if the luggage still accompanied them. As he looked past the rear of the jeep to the road behind, Hendrick experienced the first of many feelings of awe. The narrowing road, covered with pine cones, Spanish moss, and magnolia leaves, simply disappeared into the lush foliage and dense forest of this completely unspoiled setting. Though they had come but a short distance, the dock and, for that matter, civilization could have been only a memory.

Jason broke the silence. "What'll it be, Mr. Reporter, up to the north end first or the south?"

JAHEEWAH

"Where is the Institute?" Hendrick asked.

"It's more or less in the middle," Jason replied. "I thought we'd end up there."

Hendrick grinned at him and said, "Well, Jason, why don't you head this buggy north, and I'll try to stay in here with you?"

Jason laughed and gunned the jeep to the left. As they rumbled along the poorly paved road, Jason gave Hendrick an encapsulated version of how the island formed, pointing alternately toward the ocean and then back towards the mainland. Jason's knowledge of the island obviously derived from a life spent on the islands rather than from textbooks and lectures at a university. He described the estuaries and marshlands with common sense terminology and talked at length about the importance of them in the ecology of the area. Jason spoke as if he were revealing a prized possession.

"That marsh grass goes on for about seven miles up this side of the island an' then opens out in the ocean. There are more channels weavin' in an' out than you an' me got innards. When I was a kid, my daddy used to take me fishin' all through the marshes. I guess he taught me more about the islands than anybody else." A troubled look appeared on Jason's face, and he pointed to a small yacht at anchor in the river. "I don't know how long the islands goin' to be kept natural with them developers nosin' around. What they talkin' about doin' is buyin' up the north end of the island for development an' leavin' the south end for the Institute."

"Do you think they'll get it?" asked Hendrick.

"Yep. In the end they'll get it. The Institute's already hurtin' for money, an' the politicians see it as a easy way to pay for the Institute an' bring in a lot of tourist trade too. They was a big meetin' a couple of months ago with a bunch of state boys down here lookin' the place over. I think they was ready to close the deal then, but the H.I. put enough pressure on somebody to hold them off. The big problem is these people figure everythin' that happens here, happens in the sea. They don't know how much goes on right out there in the marshes—estuaries, they calls them. A lot of the fish come in an' lay their eggs. Then they

19

hatch, go out to sea, an' it all starts all over again. I tell you what—they plop some big motel out there an' the roads to get to it, you can say goodbye to the fishin' and shrimpin' around here."

Abruptly, Jason slammed on the brakes and said, "Look here!"

Hendrick looked ahead to see a huge alligator slowly crossing the road.

"That's old Tom," Jason said authoritatively. "He rules the roost up here. Wouldn't it be fun to see some fat yankee, floatin' on his inner tube, look up to see old Tom starin' him in the face?"

They both laughed, and Jason drove ahead. He continued, "In the early days they used to be a settlement up here. Them foundations over there is all that's left of the buildings but it sure must have been pretty. Old Mother Nature can claim it back in a hurry when people stay away too long."

"Can we take a closer look?"

"Sure enough."

Hendrick examined what remained of the foundations. Halves of once-square walls were now rounded by age and covered with wild vines and lichen. Occasionally, a rotting tree trunk had fallen across the walls, and no one saw the need of cleaning it all out. Glancing toward the inland waterway, he admired the untarnished beauty of the marsh grass as it changed colors in the early morning sun—shadowing in the breezes like a plush carpet. The marshes extended nearly all the way to the mainland. Hendrick looked back to the island and noticed clearings cut among the dense growth. He asked Jason, "Did they farm this area; or raise cattle here?"

"Cotton. They raised mostly cotton, an' they was a lot of black folks to farm it. Mostly slaves an' some of them West Indians brought here to work the farms. Some of the men on the island have ancestors amongst them, an' they tell about them sometimes when we all just sittin' around." Jason drove on slowly and continued, "I got somethin' else up here I want you to see."

Soon the paving stopped, and only a dirt and sand lane remained. A few minutes more and they reached the north tip of the island where the trees had thinned and the gentle surf could be heard above the idling jeep. Hendrick watched the terns and gulls as they scavenged the beach after each wave looking for food. He felt a sense of peace and quiet he had not experienced in some time. As he looked back toward the south, he saw the reason Jason had brought him here. From their position, there appeared a natural entranceway to the interior of the island. It was formed by two aged live oak trees between which they had driven. Twenty feet above the ground, a single log connected the huge trees, guarding the dirt road which passed underneath. The log lintel, at least six feet in diameter, rested securely in the gnarled forks of the massive trees.

"My God," exclaimed Hendrick. "How in the hell did that get up there?"

Jason grinned and replied, "It's a puzzle, ain't it?"

"The thing must weigh tons. What did they do, bring in a crane to lift it?"

Jason explained, "Nobody knows for sure. From the looks of it, we figure it's been up there at least a hundred years. You can see where the cross piece has been grown over by the trunk—that doesn't happen very quick. The trees themselves has been there over two hundred years. There's about as many stories as there is storytellers. Most people here think that the old Mister Randolph—he used to own the whole island—had it done. He bought the island as a family play-pretty, an' they all spent their winters here. Some people think he put it up with some sort of derrick off a ship an' then put gas lanterns up on the log for a signal or lighthouse or somethin'. They say he was bringin' in ships at night. Soon after some lights was seen, they'd be a bunch of new blacks workin' the cotton." Jason flashed an all-knowing grin and said, "Sounds right interesting, don't it?"

Hendrick agreed, "Certainly does. Have we got time to take a closer look?"

"We got all the time you want, Mr. Hendricks."

23

"Hendrick!"

"Yeah," Jason answered.

They stepped out of the jeep and walked back toward the structure. The twin oaks supporting the beam appeared as substantial as the columns of any mansion on the mainland. Hendrick walked around the trees, frequently looking up into the canopy. He remembered the last logs he lugged into his house for the fireplace.

"I guess a big enough helicopter could lift it, but I don't see how it could get it through the limbs."

"They's other explanations," Jason added.

"Like what?" asked Hendrick.

"Jaheewah."

"What?"

"Jaheewah—God of the Winds," Jason replied mysteriously.

"So that's where the name of the island came from," Hendrick commented.

"Yep. The Indians named it after one of their bird gods, an' some people today still believe Jaheewah rules the island," Jason shot a glance toward Hendrick, ". . . animals an' people alike."

Jason sat down and leaned against the huge oak. He began a narrative that Hendrick felt almost hypnotic in the telling.

"I remember the night I first heard about Jaheewah. Me an' a buddy came on the island to do some coon huntin' an' was walkin' right up here on the tip of the island when we seen a light shinin' through the trees. They was a cracklin' sound—pine cones burnin'—an' the firelight sent crazy shadows dancin'—playin' all in the woods around us. We both heard a kind of moanin' sound, an' neither of us wanted the other to call him chicken, so we kept on comin'. The closer we got, the scareder we was, but they didn't know we was watchin' them. They was a big fire right where you're standin', an' they all was dancin' around the flames. They begin kind of chantin', an' then they started yellin' like banshees: *'Jaheeeewah. Jaheeeewah.'* I tell you, it scared the doodly-squat out of both of us, an' we made it back to the dock a helluva lot faster than we got up here. When we told my daddy about it, he just laughed an' said we'd been smokin' too much grapevine."

"You think you might have just imagined it?"

"Hell no!" Jason retorted. "We seen what we seen. The next day, we was goin' fishing, so we made my daddy come out with us to prove there was somethin' here. I never will forget what we seen. We walked right here in the middle of them two trees, an' there was no trace of any fire—anywhere. My old man was about ready to kick our butts when I looked up there—at the log. Of course, the bark's all gone now, but that day, there was big gashes like someone had gotten up there with a machete knife an' whacked two big cuts in the wood. I couldn't figure it out until I heard one of the older workmen tellin' somebody he had seen Jaheewah the night before. I guessed he was one of them that was yellin' for that bird. He said they danced an' called for Jaheewah to come, an' the bird lit on that log up there to talk to them. Now, if he made those gashes with his claws, that'd give him a wingspan of about ninety feet." Jason paused, then asked rhetorically, "That's a pretty big bird, ain't it?"

"Well, I've heard of some pretty large California condors with eight feet wingspans—but you don't *really* believe all that, do you?"

"I'll just say this: I ain't seen the bird myself, but I sure seen them claw marks. There's one old man on the island who is supposed to have seen him, an' he says he's black as night an' big as the maintenance barn at the Institute. The Indians believed he comes to remove evil from the island, an' this place here was built to give him a roost to rest on before he flies off to sea with his victim."

Hendrick didn't respond for awhile. He didn't know exactly why. Of course, he didn't believe any of this "local color," but the story reached him in a way that he could neither accept nor disregard. He also began to see that Jason was himself affected by the telling of the story, and perhaps, reinforcing his own acceptance of legend versus reason. They headed back to the jeep, and neither talked much as they re-traced their drive through Jaheewah's "roost" and back into the island's interior.

For a while, they drove along the same stretch of road that had taken them to the tip of the island, but soon Jason turned the jeep onto a side road which led toward the ocean.

Hendrick had not noticed the road earlier, and he began to realize how conditioned he was to paved roads—cleanly sectioning and dissecting the land. As he was to discover many times over, nature ultimately had her way with the earth. Mounds of sand, covered with the first stretches of marsh-grass, and sea-swept vines formed the beginning of the wall separating sea and land.

The jeep wound its way through the natural barrier and emerged onto the smooth inward stretch of beach.

Low tide left a wide expanse of sun-baked sand. The sea stood calm in mid-morning, and the two men stepped out of the jeep and walked toward the surf. Hendrick sensed more strongly the solitude of this place. He wondered for a moment why he, like many others, found themselves almost involuntarily at the water's edge. Was it something more significant than just the fascination of the persistent waves and expanse of the sea? Always awed by the ocean, he felt even more so standing before it almost alone. Never before had he walked upon a beach devoid of rude diggings in the sand, discarded plastic containers or beach toys—even footprints. The ever-present gulls and terns played and fed in the mild surf. When he looked northward for the six miles or so they had traveled down the island, it appeared uninhabited. He turned to look south and was almost startled by the lone figure of a man—a single human silhouette against the limitless horizon of sky, sea, and sand. Jason noted Hendrick's surprise, and his voice interrupted the peaceful silence.

"That's old Beebo down there shellin'."

"He's a member of the Institute?"

Jason grinned. "Well, in a way he is. He ain't one of them scientists, but he's a kind of collector. We'll drive down there in a minute an' you can talk with him."

Jason reached down and lifted a flat disc from the sand.

"Here you go. I'll give you your first souvenir." He handed the sand dollar to Hendrick. "Tell you what—you let that dry out real good an' then shellac it, an' you'll have yourself a real nice play-pretty to put on your desk."

Hendrick admired the intricate design of the shell. He had seen them commercially prepared as jewelry for sale in the tourist shops. He looked again at the slowly approaching figure, holding a sack in his hand. As he watched, the man stopped walking and stood facing the ocean. He stared at the sea for a long while, then began working his way towards them again.

"Does he come out here often?"

"Every day. You can just about set your watch by him. He's a black man—got Indian blood in him, they say. Don't know how old he is, but he's been on this island all his life. Few years ago, they took him over to the mainland for

31

somethin'—to the hospital it was, I guess, then they brought him right back. Except for that time, he's spent every day of his life here."

"I'd like to talk to him if I could."

"Come on, we'll drive down there an' you can meet him."

They climbed in, and Jason headed the jeep down the beach, avoiding the occasional pools of standing water. As they neared the figure at the water's edge, Jason slowed down. He waited for the man to notice them, and when Beebo looked their way, Jason sharply turned the jeep away heading back toward the interior of the island. As Jason killed the motor, Hendrick looked at him for an explanation.

"Old Beebo is afraid of cars, so you has to let him think he's scarin' them off. He ain't figured out that people drive the things. If we'd a kept comin' toward him, he'd a just took off runnin'."

The old black man stared at the two getting out of the jeep. He grinned as he recognized Jason but eyed Hendrick suspiciously for a moment. As Jason chatted with Beebo, Hendrick examined Beebo's features and immediately planned a story on the old man. Beebo wore faded brown pants, worn through at the knees. As they talked, he frequently rubbed his hand against his leg as if drying it from the wetness of the shells. His laceless shoes as well as the cuffs of his trousers were wet from the surf. His jacket, worn over a dark work shirt, was frayed at the sleeves and elbows—the front held together by two large safety pins. Hendrick thought him a dark man in ways other than just color. His hands were wrinkled and toughened by long hours in the sun. He removed his cap, and rubbed his leathery brow with his sleeve. His hair matched the silvery grayness of the stubble on his face. Hendrick looked at his eyes. They seemed to float in an abundant liquid in the sockets and penetrated Hendrick in an intriguing and foreboding way. Hendrick could only imagine what they had seen or even now what they were transmitting to the old man's brain.

"Hey, Beebo! How you gettin' along today?"

"Yeh!" answered the old man. "I picking up the shells—see?" He held the brown paper sack open for them to inspect and looked at Jason and Hendrick for approval. "You see? I pick up all the shells I find."

"This is Mr. Hendricks, Beebo. He wants to talk to you sometime. How about that?" Hendrick started to correct Jason again about his name but dismissed it as futile.

Beebo grinned broadly at Hendrick. "I talk all the time . . . to lots of people. I like talk." He paused for a few seconds, then repeated, "I like talk. I like pick up all the shells."

"How long have you lived on the island, Beebo?" Hendrick asked.

The man stared curiously at Hendrick as if waiting for further explanation of his question. Then he suddenly smiled and said, "I live here all the time." He turned toward the south. "I live over there—in a house an' . . . an' it all mine. I come to the water all the time an' I pick up all the shells—you see?" He held up the sack again for their inspection.

"That's good, Beebo. That's real good. Ain't that good, Mr. Hendricks?"

"Yes," Hendrick answered. "That's good, Beebo."

Beebo smiled proudly then abruptly turned to stare at the ocean as he had done when alone. After a few seconds, Jason spoke to Beebo but, knowing what Beebo's response would be, he looked directly at Hendrick.

"What are you lookin' for, Beebo?"

"I look Jaheewah. Jaheewah come to island—from far away. I see Jaheewah some time an' tell all the people Jaheewah come."

"That's right, Beebo. You let us know when old Jaheewah come." Jason reached down to pick up a shell and handed it to the old man. Beebo took the shell, looked at it, then dropped it on the sand. He glanced at them enigmatically then wandered on up the beach.

"So long, Beebo," Jason said. "See you tomorrow." Both men watched the old man amble away from them to continue his persistent search for shells. Jason explained that Beebo was one of several permanent residents who had been living on the island even before the Institute was established.

"The man's crazy," Hendrick said after he was sure Beebo couldn't hear them.

Jason replied, "Maybe just a little. But he ain't gonna hurt nobody"

"How long has he been doing this—I mean, does he spend his whole day collecting shells?"

"Just about. When he gets hisself a sack full he takes them over to the Institute."

"What was wrong with the shell you gave him?"

"Wrong kind." Jason reached into his pocket for another shell. "He picks up these here. They calls them 'olives.' " He handed the cylindrical shell to Hendrick. "They hard to find sometimes."

"I can't get over that. The man's crazy as a loon and he's wandering around—anywhere he wants to go."

"Well, just what would you do with him?"

"Hell, I don't know. But surely there's a rest home or some place on the mainland. He could get himself in trouble out here alone."

"You put old Beebo in some nursing home an' you'd *really* have trouble on your hands. Out here, he's happy an' free an' doin' his job."

"But what happens when he runs out of shells?"

"He don't run out of shells."

"But you said they were hard to find."

"They is. But they plenty here because the H.I. has some thrown on the beach after old Beebo quits walkin' every day."

"You mean Beebo brings them into the Institute, and the Head of the Institute brings them back out here?"

"Yep. That's the way it works."

"That's the craziest thing I ever heard."

"Let me ask you, Mr. Hendricks. Did Beebo look okay to you? Did he seem pretty happy?"

"I imagine so."

"I know so. He's a helluva lot happier out here doing his job an' takin' care of hisself than he would be wastin' away on the front porch of some old folks home. An' as far as he knows, he's gettin' things done an' helpin' out Doc Farrow. The H.I. knows what would happen to him, so he's seen to it old Beebo has hisself a job to do. Now, don't you imagine fifteen minutes of scatterin' sea shells on the beach ain't too much trouble if it gives Beebo something he can take pride in? If a man don't have pride, he don't have nothin', whether he's crazy or not. Besides, I think we all a little bit crazy anyhow."

Hendrick watched Beebo walking away from them. For a fleeting moment, he almost envied him his carefree life wandering along the beach. Though he had not met Farrow, he was developing an increased respect for him. Farrow's fight for the preservation of the island appealed to Hendrick's sense of purpose as well as his sympathy for the underdog. The more he thought of Beebo's plight, the more he admired Farrow's simple and humane solution. He was anxious to meet this man.

"I guess it's a pretty good life for him after all," Hendrick admitted.

Jason and Hendrick continued their ride around the southern tip of the island. The paved road they traveled roughly followed the circumference of the island, and returned them into the complex of buildings which housed the barracks, laboratories, administration building, infirmary, and maintenance barns.   "Just so you know, if you get into trouble, you can check yourself in over there at the infirmary. Doc Palliston is there all the time. He'll take good care of you."

Jason stopped the jeep in front of a building with clapboard siding and tiled roof which Jason identified as one of the laboratories. A young girl, dressed in jeans and a lab jacket, stood at the doorway of the building. She was talking with an older man, distinguished by a deep tan, greying hair, and an unusual carved meerschaum pipe held adroitly out of the corner of his mouth.

"I see Doc Farrow's here to meet you."

JAHEEWAH

As Jason and Hendrick approached, Farrow greeted them enthusiastically.

"Welcome to Jaheewah, Mr. Hendrick. I hope you'll forgive my not meeting you at the dock. Has Jason shown you around properly?"

"Yes, he has. Thank you very much, Jason. I enjoyed it."

"You're welcome." Jason pointed across the courtyard to another building. "I'll set your things on the porch over there—them's the barracks. They be alright. It was a real pleasure meetin' you, Mr. Hendricks. I imagine I'll be runnin' into you later."

"Right. Thanks again."

Farrow nodded approvingly to Jason then spoke to Hendrick.

"Mr. Hendrick, I want you to meet Margaret Courtney. She's our prettiest lab assistant—at least in this building." The girl smiled and held out her hand to Hendrick. "Margaret, this is Robert Hendrick of the *Courier*. He's

40

going to be with us for a while to do a series of articles on the Institute."

"How do you do, Mr. Hendrick?"

"It's Bob, okay?"

"Sure," she replied.

Farrow continued, "Bob, I regret that I can't take you through the laboratories myself right now. I've got a meeting with the administrative staff in about ten minutes. I've asked Margaret if she would do the honors."

"Of course. I don't want to cause any inconvenience."

"Not at all. Now, dinner is served at six, and I would like for you to join us at our table, if you will."

"I'll be happy to. Thanks very much."

"Then, I'll say goodbye for now and see you this evening. Perhaps tomorrow we can have a nice long chat about how we can be of assistance while you're on the island. Oh

yes, anyone at the barracks can show you your room. Well
. . . if you'll excuse me—and thanks, Margaret."

She smiled at Farrow—more out of courtesy than af-
fection, Hendrick thought—then Farrow left. Had anyone
asked, Hendrick would have admitted to a subtle feeling of
being temporarily shelved for Farrow's convenience. But
he quickly dismissed the thought from his mind as Margaret suggested they begin their tour.

"Bob, I'll show you the labs first—right in here."

The doorway led into a small foyer on the walls of
which hung bulletin boards. A set of double swinging
doors led into a long room which served as one laboratory.
The smell of the room reminded him of his high school
chemistry lab—a pungent contrast to the fresh sea air he
had been absorbing for the past hour. Margaret described
the function of this particular lab and occasionally asked
students to explain what they were doing.

"Basically, this lab is designated for environmental
studies. We take daily water and sediment samples and
run tests on them here. In the estuaries, there are inflows
of both seawater and freshwater which create an amazing

amount of nutrients in the water and sediment. The result of this activity makes estuaries the most productive natural habitats in the world. We watch for dramatic changes in saline content and monitor bacteria levels. If there were some toxins or threats of pollution, it would show up here pretty quickly." Hendrick remembered Jason's earlier comment about the importance of the estuaries: *". . . people figure everything that happens here, happens in the sea. They don't know how much goes on right out there in the marshes."*

Hendrick remarked, "I expected to see a lot of tanks full of strange-looking fish."

"You'll see that in the other lab. Among other things, we have tests running on shellfish and crustaceans in there. Actually, we study just about every species of marine life forms indigenous to this area. We can see those now if you like—it's a little more interesting in there. We'll go through those doors and across the hall that connects with the other buildings.

"The lecture hall we pass through used to be a small theatre just for the Randolph family and their guests. It works very nicely for us now. The senior residents lecture there, and it's all set up with a projection booth and large screen for slides and special films or video. Did Jason tell you about the Randolphs?"

"Yeah, he gave me a little background on them."

In the other lab, Margaret identified most of the fish in the test tanks and described the studies in progress. Hendrick noticed that unlike the environmental lab, this one contained four enclosed areas along one wall. Three of them were clearly in use. The larger of the four, however, was noticeably unequipped. The shelves were empty, and only an old wooden desk and a filing cabinet remained.

"What about this area?"

"That was Dr. Stassen's private lab. Unfortunately, he drowned last week, and all of his materials were moved out, and tests were stopped."

"Oh, so he's the one I read about in an old paper this morning on the boat. Did you know him very well?"

"Pretty well—I was his lab assistant."

"Oh, I see." Hendrick attributed her hesitancy and obvious discomfort in talking about Stassen to some personal closeness to the man and decided to temporarily drop the subject.

Margaret continued, "If we go through here, I can show you our museum."

Another set of doors led into a long, narrow hallway. Along the walls, a series of wood and glass display cases housed a variety of artifacts which had been found on the island. An impressive arrangement of arrowheads and other Indian tools caught Hendrick's eye. Adjacent to them were various sizes of sharks' teeth; each was labeled to identify the type and age of the specimen. Next came an assortment of snakes beautifully preserved in glass jars which also were clearly identified.

"The stuffed birds, I think, are the highlight of the collection. A man on the mainland had collected these all his life, and just before he died, he donated them to the Institute."

Hendrick had seen nothing like this before. Nearly ten cases were filled with expertly stuffed birds in natural settings. A progression in size led from the smallest little finch to an osprey the size of which astounded Hendrick. Noting the meticulous preservation of the colors and markings of the birds, Hendrick was awed by the range and variety of the bird world.

"There was so little killing of birds on the island, it had become a natural sanctuary. Some of the Audubon people spent weeks here. They told us that they had spotted and catalogued over 200 species of birds."

"Some of these are just outlandish—like that one there. The colors are fantastic."

"Yeah. Nature does alright. Well, that's it, Bob. I imagine Dr. Farrow will show you the Administration Building later."

"Right. Thanks for the excellent tour, Margaret. I enjoyed it."

"Good. I'm glad."

"See you later—at dinner?"

"Yeah. I'll be there. I've got something coming off the centrifuge, so I need to get back."

"Okay. I had better find my room and get settled in. Thanks again, Margaret."

"You're welcome. 'Bye."

Hendrick left the building and walked across the well-kept courtyard toward the barracks. A few young students passed him and nodded politely. Hendrick smiled and continued on his way to the barracks. Soon after finding his room, Hendrick discovered hallway vending machines and bought hot coffee and a sandwich for his lunch.

Like most of the buildings on the island, the wood-frame barracks had served another purpose prior to the acquisition of the island by the state. Originally, the building was used as a stable for horses. Jason had told him that Mr. Randolph had imported a variety of riding horses used for hunting wild boar and deer and also for pleasure riding on the beaches. The courtyard had been a small paddock where Randolph proudly exhibited the magnificent animals for guests.

JAHEEWAH

Each room in the barracks was about the size of three adjacent stalls and was furnished with a steel bed with springs and a mattress, study table and lamp, two chairs, and an old fabric rug. The rooms had a single door and two small windows with venetian blinds. Hendrick opened one window, raised the blinds, and felt a soft breeze, cooled by the shade of the tall pines which surrounded and protected the building.

Hendrick hung his clothes in the improvised closet, a single rod stretched between the wall and a partition by the doorway. He then put his typewriter and a ream of paper on the desk. He decided to log an hour or so recounting the morning's activities and his first impressions of the island and the Institute. Through years of writing, he had established a technique that usually worked well for him. He would quickly get a few paragraphs on his notepad, even though they frequently would not appear in a second draft. Just having something there was enough to get him past the blank page. After a couple of hours, he stretched out on the bed and almost fell asleep. The fragrance of the sea pines and the strikingly loud and varied bird calls permeated the room. Glancing at his watch, he realized that dinner would be served soon, so he found the communal bathroom, washed his face, and changed into a fresh shirt before walking to the dining hall.

Inside the building, Hendrick noticed that most of the tables were filled, and he hesitated momentarily looking for a convenient place to sit. Farrow, seated at a large table, saw Hendrick and stood to motion him to an empty seat. Hendrick nodded appreciatively and, after gathering plates, glassware, and utensils on his tray, joined Farrow and the others. Farrow extended his hand to Hendrick.

"Welcome, Mr. Hendrick. Won't you please join us?"

"Yes, thank you." Hendrick took his seat, and Farrow made a quick, informal introduction of all those seated at the table.

Hendrick found the meal surprisingly good. Dinner was served family style—a salad, then platters of fried chicken, bowls of potatoes and vegetables, and homemade biscuits. Hendrick made a comment about the quality and quantity of the food, and Farrow assured him that the rustic conditions of the island did not inhibit good, southern cooking.

"If I thought I could get away with it, I'd pay our cooks more than anyone else. They keep most of us quite contented." Pointing to the man on Hendrick's left, he continued, "This is Sherman's fifth year on the island, and I finally realized that it's the food that keeps him here."

"No, he's got his eye on a good-looking alligator on the south end of the island," snapped one of the other men at the table. They all laughed, and conversations continued in smaller groups.

After refills of hot coffee, the group gradually dispersed until only Hendrick, Farrow, and one of the men he had met on the boat remained. The conversation was very relaxed with an exchange of questions regarding the island Institute and Farrow's expectations for the articles. Farrow provided a short description of the local history of the island, his hopes for the Institute, the difficulties in keeping it solvent, and the importance of their work globally. Soon, Farrow and his colleagues excused themselves and Hendrick returned to his room.

As he lay in bed thinking over the conversations he had had during the day, Hendrick remembered that Margaret Courtney had not appeared in the dining hall, or at least he had not noticed her. He dismissed her absence as unimportant—something that probably occurred often with these people.

Hendrick had just put his notepad down when a sound at his door disturbed him. As he got up from the squeaky steel bed, he heard footsteps hurrying down the hall. By the time he opened his door, the hallway was vacant, a bare light bulb providing the only light. Hendrick stood in his doorway a moment longer. Returning to bed, he thought to himself, *"I guess my visitor changed his mind."*

Despite the interruption, he found it very easy to get to sleep and, much to his surprise, did not awaken until nearly eight-thirty the next morning.

JAHEEWAH

CHAPTER 3

After breakfast and an interview with two of the newest students at the Institute, Hendrick returned to his room. He spent the remainder of the morning knocking out a piece on the history of the island and the influence of the Institute and its personnel area.

Arriving at the dining hall for lunch, Hendrick saw Margaret Courtney eating alone. He joined her, and they talked until both needed to get to other tasks. She puzzled him. Their conversation was comfortable, but he sensed something about her he could not quite identify. His sensitivity had occasionally confused other situations, and he had even been told as a student that his work might improve if he were not so subjective. *"You can speculate all you want, but as a reporter, you must simply state what happened or what was said, and let the readers decide for themselves what's going on."*

"Bob? Do you think . . ." she hesitated, apprehensively, Hendrick thought, but continued nonchalantly, "Uh . . . did you bring an umbrella? It's going to pour buckets in about two minutes."

"Actually, I did. But of course, it's back in the room. Maybe it won't last too long. You know, I've never figured out if you get wetter running or walking. You don't know, do you? I mean, you're a scientist!" They laughed. Several times in their conversation, she appeared about to ask him something but hesitated and then went another direction. It wasn't shyness or simply being coy—but it was there, he concluded. The wind began to pick up, and then a clap of thunder startled them. A gentle rain accompanied each of them to their destination—her to the lab and him to his room.

The afternoon rain lasted only a half-hour or so, but its lingering moisture heightened the sweet, fragrant mixture of crepe myrtle and azaleas. Hendrick had spent the time since lunch re-editing his text and typing a clean copy to be mailed to his office. He had arranged to have the Institute secretary copy each article and send it on to his editor.

Hendrick glanced out the single window of his room. Warm, red light of a magnificent sunset bathed the courtyard and the surrounding tile-roofed buildings of the complex. To the west and the mainland beyond, there appeared striking silhouettes created by gnarled and twisting limbs of aged live oaks, delicately draped by ghostly Spanish moss. No human sound could be heard. The oncoming darkness was filled by mysterious calls of night creatures— louder here because of their abundance and the natural quietness of the environment.

Toward the ocean, a red glow appeared on the black horizon, and soon thereafter, the crackling sound of fire could just barely be heard above the surf. Hendrick had been standing outside the barracks awaiting the jeep that would take him and others to the beach party that evening. In the distance, he heard the jeep, and Jason quickly arrived at the barracks. Hendrick greeted Jason and climbed into the front seat, bracing himself for the rough ride to the ocean. The low tree limbs bordering the sand and dirt road to the beach reached out as if to grab them as Jason maneuvered the vehicle quickly on the winding lane. As they reached the tall dunes protecting the inner island, the glow of the fire shone more brightly, illuminating several figures darting in and out of the surf. When they cleared the dunes and drove onto the beach, Hendrick felt the warmth of the fire that was fueled by tree stumps and other debris strewn upon the sand. Jason parked the jeep nearby and began to unload several folding canvas stools, food and beer, and freshly cut poles for roasting wieners. Soon, groups of three and four gathered around the fire to devour the supplies. To Hendrick, they seemed different as a group than they had originally appeared to him. In the laboratories, they were young and, in some cases, obviously brilliant scientists. Here on the beach at night, the frivolous conversation, the camaraderie, and the good-natured, teasing one-upsmanship reminded Hendrick of fraternity parties at college where inhibitions were left at home and newer students were nervously attempting to establish their status in the group.

Afterwards, when most had finished eating and the chill of the sea breezes urged them closer to the fire, a guitar appeared, and all joined in singing familiar folk songs. The strains of *"Bridge Over Troubled Water"* and James Taylor's *"You've Got A Friend"* were perfect for the occasion. Hendrick felt a degree of contentment in the pleasantness of the evening and warmth of the fire. Joy Martin, an attractive girl of twenty who had been softly strumming the guitar, was urged to sing songs she had no doubt performed often for this group. Most were songs of love and sadness, nature and beauty, or even death and war. Joy, dressed in jeans and a windbreaker, entertained with confidence and sincerity. She seemed shy except when she sang. Hendrick found her embarrassed gratitude for the applause charming. Her music, enhanced by the simplicity and beauty of the guitar's plaintive tones, became, in itself, accompaniment to evening sea winds, the lapping waves of the constant surf, and the crackling of fresh firewood tossed onto the red hot coals. Hendrick glanced around the campfire, trying to put names to faces, when he noticed that the young man seated next to Margaret Courtney rose, said something to her, and joined another group nearby. She made no effort to follow him. Her eyes were focused on the fire as Hendrick approached. She continued watching the burning embers as he sat beside her.

"Hello, there."

She turned slowly and responded, "Hi."

"How are you doing?"

"Okay, I guess."

"I'd like to join you, but I don't want to impose on your date," he said pointing with his coffee cup towards the boy who had just left her.

57

"That's alright. He's not my date."

"Can I get you something? A hot dog, or coffee, or some beer?"

"No thanks," she answered quickly. "Well . . . maybe some coffee would be nice."

Hendrick went to the table nearby for the coffee and glanced back at the girl. She stared into the fire. As he returned, she looked up and smiled politely. "Thanks," she said, carefully taking the coffee mug from him. They sat quietly for a moment or two, sipping the coffee and looking into the fire. In the firelight, Hendrick found her very attractive, and her reticent manner intrigued him.

"Tell me, Miss Courtney, where is your home?"

"Is this for the record?" she asked teasingly.

"No, not at all. I'm sorry. Did it sound that way?"

"Well, I'm not used to the 'Miss Courtney' bit—except from Dr. Farrow at times."

Hendrick laughed and offered his hand. "I've been on the paper too long. Let's start again. Bob and Margaret, okay?"

She smiled and took his hand. He held hers a moment longer than necessary and said, "Friends, okay?"

"Okay." She withdrew her hand from his but smiled at him as she did so. Teasingly, she asked in a husky, serious voice, "Tell me, Bob, how do you like the island?"

They both laughed and she seemed more relaxed and comfortable.

"Seriously, where is your home?" he asked.

"Syracuse. But my folks moved down to Miami, and then I got the assignment here."

"It's nice that you can be a little closer to them. Are they both in good health?"

"Yeah, they're fine. But it's not that much closer, and I don't go down there that much."

"Do you like it here?"

"Yes and no. Mostly yes, I guess. I enjoy the work and the research and particularly the atmosphere. I mean . . . I like the quietness and the solitude when you want it."

"Yeah, I know. So far, I like it here very much. This may shock you, but I really don't miss Charleston's buses and trolleys, and sirens, and people screaming at each other. I'm afraid that my boss thought I should only be here a day or so and will be calling me back soon. I told him this morning that I was on to something—sort of an angle—and it would probably be a week before I would wrap it up." Margaret's sudden change of expression suggested to him that he had struck some nerve. He had intended nothing more than pleasant conversation. He had noticed in his first encounter with her a kind of analytical alertness he saw in her eyes. Perhaps it was the scientist in her, but to him, there seemed a quickness both in perception and thought, as if she were struggling with some scientific mystery or puzzle—trying to sort it out logically. He had also wondered just what her relationship with Dr. Stassen had been. How close were they? These observations by Hendrick, took all of three seconds, and she interrupted his musings.

"How are your articles coming along?"

Watching her closely, Hendrick had not intended to push her just yet about Stassen's death. He quickly decided that now wasn't the time. "Fine! You people are doing some really interesting things here. You know what just amazed me was the collection of birds in the museum. The colors and size of some of them fascinated me."

"It is a very well done collection. And the nice thing is that nearly all of them have been seen on the island."

"Even Jaheewah?" Hendrick teased.

"Not by me."

"Do you believe the bird exists?"

She turned to him, eyeing him incredulously, "Are you kidding?"

"Yeah, I guess so. How long have you worked out here?"

"Actually, this is my third summer, but I graduated last spring, so I'm planning to stay all of this next year. Dr. Farrow has assured me of a position—perhaps working directly with him."

"Do you enjoy working for Farrow? I mean, do you think he's a good administrator?" Again she hesitated before speaking, choosing her words carefully, Hendrick thought.

61

"I'm actually not that close to him, so I don't have definite feelings about the man. I really feel like I'm working for myself—you know? Like on my own projects. And Farrow's job is something else. I think I would have to say he's a good administrator."

"That's kind of the relationship I have with my editor. I mean, he does read everything, but I write what I want to write and unless I'm really out in left field, he'll run the story pretty much like I wrote it, and he'll back me on it."

"Have you ever gotten in trouble with anything you've written?"

"You mean with the editor?"

"Yeah."

"Well, I almost did once. It was one of those deals where I thought I had enough information on a local city official to really nail him. My editor kept pressing me to reveal the source of my information to him. I wouldn't do it at first. I began lecturing *him* about freedom of the press and investigative reporting techniques, and he just started laughing. He led me to believe that my article was already in print. But, he got real serious and told me that if I had any inclination towards remaining in the newspaper business, I should learn to double- or triple-check my sources. Somehow or another, he had discovered who was feeding me information and knew that I was being set up and that the allegations were questionable at best. He let me think on that for a while, and after a long silence when we just looked at each other, he told me that he had pulled the story. He explained that had he not caught it, we would have done an accusatory article citing criminal acts, and the man would have sued and won. It was a sobering experience that I won't forget."

"Isn't it terribly frustrating when you think, or even know, something's happened but can't prove it?"

"Yes. But you've always got to be able to prove it or it's no good—true or not."

"Well, I'm glad I'm not a reporter. I wouldn't like digging for dirt in people's lives." Her comment revealed an aspect of her character more than it seemed directed toward Hendrick personally. Yet he found himself somewhat defensive.

"I know. But the alternatives are political payoffs, conspiracies, and cover-ups. It's sticky at times, but if what you're investigating is important, then usually the right people suffer, and it's best for everyone else in the long run." He paused then added, "I'm sorry. I didn't want to get off on the newspaper business.

"How about more coffee?" Hendrick offered.

"No, no thanks. I think Jason is ready to take some people back to the barracks, and I believe I'll go on back now. It's been a long day."

"May I see you home?"

"Thanks, but I'll just ride back with them."

They stood, and she threw the cold coffee into the fire and placed the mug in the wash bucket at the serving table.

"Margaret?" He touched her arm gently to stop her. "I'm not going to pull any punches with you. I really enjoyed talking with you tonight and I'd like to again— perhaps over dinner and wine someplace. But I also want to talk with you about some other things. Just things I'm curious about and I don't want you to get the two confused. May I talk with you on that basis sometime?"

She looked at him for several seconds before answering.

"Yeah . . . sure. And I think I'd like very much to have dinner with you sometime."

She covered his hand with hers momentarily then pulled away to walk towards the jeep, leaving him standing by the slowly dying fire. He watched the vehicle rumble off the beach and into the darkness. Several people remained, and he decided to have more coffee. The thought occurred to him that he had not noticed Farrow the whole evening.

The smell of the food reminded him that he had not eaten. There were still a few hot dogs and some potato salad left. He fixed a plate and quickly devoured the food. By the time Hendrick had eaten and talked with a few of the students still gathered around the fire, Jason had returned with the jeep and was busily fixing his own plate of food. Hendrick looked around again for Farrow and approached Jason who was leaning nonchalantly against the jeep with less than half a hot dog in his hand, the result of one bite.

Jason smiled and nodded to Hendrick.

"Get enough to eat, Mr. Hendricks?"

"I've had all I wanted." Gesturing toward the fire and activity, he added, "This is a nice thing to do. Is this Farrow's party or just a get-together? I haven't seen him."

"That's because he ain't here tonight. Sometimes he comes an' sometimes he don't."

"I see." Hendrick sipped his coffee and listened to the gentle surf spilling rhythmically onto the beach. Occasionally, a burst of laughter or a chorus of a song disrupted the soft whistling sea breezes and crackling pine logs spewing sparks into the cool night air. Hendrick and Jason talked for a while longer. Hendrick found Jason to be, in his own way, an affable and adroit conversationalist. His distinctive slow drawl complemented the usual unhurried demeanor so typical of the local people Hendrick had met. Moreover, Hendrick had discovered that the slower pace of locals' conversation was also infectious. He felt certain that just these few days on the island had already affected his own speech and eased the pressure he often felt at the newspaper. He even had developed an acceptance of Jason's dubbing him incorrectly "Hendricks" as a kind of flattering nickname only Jason used. Strangely, he now looked forward to it. Jason placed his empty beer can in a trash barrel in the back of the jeep.

"Mr. Hendricks, most of the kids will find their own way back to the barracks, so if you want to ride back with me, I'm about ready to go."

"Yeah, I guess I will. Do we need to clean up around here? I'm glad to help."

"The kids usually do it an' put out the fire an' everythin', so we can go on if you're ready. I ain't rushin' you now if you want to stay longer." Jason lifted another sack of trash into the jeep, and they got in. The jeep's engine roared to life, and Jason slowly headed toward the dirt lane leading into the woods.

They soon reached the barracks. It would have been a tricky walk for someone unfamiliar with the road. Tree branches lay in the roadway, and stepping on large pine-cones could easily turn an ankle. In his room, Hendrick began some re-editing of his writing of the afternoon's work. He felt good about the article and grateful for his own awakened interest in the marine environment. He became sleepy and decided to finish the story first thing in the morning.

Lying in bed, he began to think about Margaret Courtney. She wasn't beautiful, he thought—just damned attractive. And he did want to see her on a personal basis. She interested him. He thought back over their brief conversation, and something she had said began to nag at him. *"What was it she said?"* he thought. At the time, it hadn't registered. And then he remembered: *"Isn't it frustrating when you know something's happened but can't prove it?"* He even remembered the curious expression on her face as she said it. Was it just idle conversation, or had something indeed happened that she knew about but was frightened of revealing? Contemplating this innuendo kept him awake for a little while longer, but he became drowsy and soon fell asleep

CHAPTER 4

It was Hendrick's fourth day on the island, and the dinner hour had settled into a more informal and natural routine. His presence did not seem to affect the atmosphere at
the table as he sensed it first did, and conversation usually
included him.

All through the meal, Hendrick scrutinized each of
those seated at the table. In some of the staff interviews,
he had received polite cooperation, but the length of these
sessions was sometimes abruptly shortened on the pre-
tense of lab work. In the case of a few of the senior residents, he noticed a clear reticence relating to Stassen's
death—a fact that he could not leave alone but must consider as possible complicity. Consequently, his conversations—his questions particularly with the senior residents—had become more pointed and investigative.

As they continued eating, Hendrick retreated into the shell of his mind where he began a series of mental notes: *nothing to suggest foul play, a definite feeling that something was being kept from him, Stassen was hard to work with, a very private person, and intolerant of stupidity or incompetence.*

Seated across from him at the long table, Margaret Courtney sat quietly. From things she had said, she seemed close to the old man. If Stassen was murdered, Hendrick could not see her involved. *Maybe she does know something and is afraid to tell it.* As Stassen's student assistant, she would certainly have been close enough to observe anything that might have happened in the lab.

A burst of laughter drew him back as Farrow and the others were swapping stories. Hendrick watched Farrow intently. Though dominating the informal conversation, Farrow listened with interest to the others. Their mutual respect was evident. From what Hendrick had discovered of Stassen's personality, he must not have enjoyed the same rapport. The conversation grew more serious and centered around the future of the Institute. Now, only Farrow talked.

"I really can't say. A lot depends on what happens in the legislature. In an election year, they're all running scared, and any sort of economic cut that they can brag about might be an issue to get them re-elected. We've got friends there, but most of them are young and not able to affect much change in policy. The others—it's a matter of playing their kind of cards, and sometimes we're able to do it and sometimes not. Aside from one trump I have, the only thing I've been able to do is keep reminding them and, more importantly, the public that we're down here in their interest." Nodding politely toward Hendrick, he continued, "That's why Mr. Hendrick from the *Courier* is here— to tell our public the interesting and valuable things we are doing." Hendrick smiled and nodded in return to Farrow's reference. Farrow added, "So . . . if you all are not doing anything interesting or valuable, I suggest you get your ass—pardon me, Margaret—in gear and do something interesting and valuable." They all laughed. "Because," he continued, "if you don't, we'll have another delegation down from the capital and it will be all over."

"What was that all about?" Hendrick interrupted.

"Well, I got a call one day that the following weekend I should expect three of our Senators for a tour of the Institute and that I 'naturally' would want to give them VIP treatment. They would be flown to the island by helicopter. Because of the trees, they would land on the north beach, and we were to meet them with the van. Well, I called a friend at the capital to find out what had prompted the visit. He said that the Senators were a 'select' committee appointed by the Governor to advise him of the feasibility of maintaining the island as a research center. They were nothing more than a hatchet committee to shut us down. The rationale was that after the decision to abandon the Institute, no one could complain that there had not been direct evaluation of the island and its operation. Those three wanted to make this island a tourist attraction—so I let them soak up some sun. I gave them about an hour or so then sent the van for them. Old Senator Yarborough came down here as gray as the building he sat his fat ass in. But he went back looking like a lobster." Hendrick laughed with the rest of them until he remembered that he himself had been kept waiting a little while at the dock. One of the younger students interjected, "Maybe you should have let Stassen talk to them." Instinctively, several around the table glanced toward Farrow whose expression and quick look at the student revealed an irritation about his comment. Margaret Courtney, however, looked directly at Hendrick, and he quickly caught her eye. For a brief moment, the two stared at each other before she glanced away, shifting her attention to her hands and the paper napkin she had been folding and refolding during the conversation. Hendrick continued to watch her—wondering what her look meant and if she would return his gaze. Farrow looked at his watch and broke the brief silence.

"Well, I've got a desk full of paperwork waiting—if you all will excuse me?"

They all stood, and before Hendrick could get to her, Margaret had stepped outside and was gone. Dark clouds which had brought the long rain that afternoon remained. He saw no point in trying to follow her through the darkness and decided to go on to his room. Several events of the evening intrigued him. And he wanted to think them through.

Hendrick left the dining hall and made his way in the dark through the old courtyard toward the barracks. Glancing upward through the moss-draped live oak trees, he stumbled on the edge of the concrete walkway surrounding the old fountain in the center of the courtyard. As he stooped to rub his injured foot, he heard a strange rustling sound in the trees bordering the northern end of the complex. Without warning, there was a rush of air just above his head accompanied by a loud, piercing screech shattering the quietness of the night. Hendrick crouched instinctively to withstand an attack, but the creature lit gracefully on the central pillar of the fountain. A break in the clouds spilled bright moonlight over the courtyard. Hendrick, looking at the perched bird, was awed by its size. The two just stared at each other for what seemed to Hendrick ten minutes before the bird slowly stretched his wings and lifted himself majestically off the fountain and out towards the beach. Slightly unnerved, Hendrick, astonished by the bird's power, understood more easily the superstition such a creature could generate in a suggestible mentality. In the moonlight, he could see clearly now and made his way to the doorway at the end of the barracks. As he entered the building, the hallway lights temporarily blinded him. Not enough, however, to mask the figure darting out of the building at the opposite end of the hall. Hendrick hurried to the entrance, but whoever it was had disappeared into the night.

"Aw, come on," he said under his breath, *"Cut this out."*

He walked back to his room and opened the door. Going to the desk to switch on the lamp, he quickly surveyed the room for any sign of disturbance. Seeing none, he closed the door, sat down at the desk, and paged through his legal pad to scan some notes he had taken that afternoon. He hesitated momentarily to get into his mind a clear picture of the encounter in the hall. He chided himself for being suspicious and dismissed it temporarily from thought.

Hendrick began typing again but was distracted by laughter just outside his room. Curious about the mysterious visitor in the hallway, he opened his door and saw Walt Matthews and another man standing at Matthews's door. Walt greeted him warmly.

"Oh, hello Hendrick."

"Hi. How's it going?" Hendrick replied casually.

"We're going to open a couple of beers." He opened his door and motioned Hendrick in. "You're welcome to join us if you like."

"Thanks, I will." Hendrick turned and shut the door to his room then entered the one across the hallway. Inside, Matthews's room reminded Hendrick of a counselor's quarters at a scout camp, a retreat from the pressure and responsibility of children, and equipped for "emergencies" such as a downpour which would force all the kiddies to stay in their tents. Matthews's furnishings included a brick and board bookrack with everything from science fiction and textbooks to current paperback novels. A nearby table supported an impressive stereo system. Beneath the table sat a small electric icebox, from which Matthews took three cans of beer. Matthews motioned Hendrick to a chair at the small study table and handed him a beer. Tanned from long hours in the sun, Matthews was a big man, well over six feet tall. His uncombed blond hair, falling over his ears slightly, suffered from infrequent and amateurish barbering. He had an almost continual broad grin on his face and tended to sound somewhat pretentious.

"Have a seat. It's Bob, isn't it?"

"You got it."

"Did you meet Glen, here? Glen Borden?"

"Yes, I remember from the other day."

He reached forward to shake hands with the other man, a smaller, less loquacious version of Matthews. Borden wore wire-rimmed glasses and a neatly trimmed beard and, like Matthews, had on jeans and a sport shirt. A nervous habit of his struck Hendrick right away. Borden was almost constantly moving—either crossing or uncrossing his legs and slowly rotating the beer can in his hands.

"Nice to see you," Hendrick said.

"Same here," Borden replied.

Borden had taken the only other chair in the room, and Matthews, popping open a can of beer, sat crossways on his bed, his back against the wall. Their conversation took the form of a friendly get-acquainted, welcome to Jaheewah session with Hendrick asking mostly innocuous questions about their work at the Institute. Matthews dominated the impromptu meeting—talking at length about life on the island. Hendrick thought that he and Matthews were about the same age when Matthew mentioned that he had been on Jaheewah for the past four years. Hendrick noticed that Matthews obviously enjoyed welcoming a newcomer—demonstrating his own knowledge of the island, offering to provide fun or relaxation as if he were an activities chairman. Though somewhat amused by his own "resortless" image of the island, Hendrick didn't mind the "welcome to Jaheewah" monologue. At least it afforded him an unguarded, informal view of the people who made up the Institute.

"It's not so bad here," said Matthews. "The food is great, and we occasionally have clambakes on the beach. Sometimes, Farrow will spring for renting really great movies."

"Yeah?" snapped Borden. "Like the one last month?"

"Hell, that was a mistake."

"That's what Farrow said, but I'll believe a lot of things before I'll buy that."

Matthews explained to Hendrick, "You see, one of the girls here is a real film buff, and she kept hounding Farrow to order really first-rate films—even gave him a catalog. These were real films—16 mm—which we would show in the lecture hall, the old theatre. Well, she trapped him in the dining hall, and I guess he got tired of listening to her. So, in front of all of us, he said she could choose the film. Well, right then and there, she told him for starters to get *Rebecca*—a 1940 Hitchcock film. When the film came, it was *Rebecca Of Sunnybrook Farm*. Farrow didn't say a word and just ran it on the screen. That really hacked her off, but we all sat there and watched that dumb flick."

"Yeah, and Farrow just grinned and chuckled to himself through the whole damn thing. I thought it was a crummy thing to do. I mean, she *really* loves films."

"Well, he apologized and promised to order whatever she wanted this month."

"Big deal!"

"Maybe you guys can help me out," Hendrick interjected. "I'm really having a hard time getting a clear perspective on Farrow. I'm sure you know that, to some people, financing the project here isn't always justified and that I'm here to do favorable stories on the Institute. Now, if I portray the Head of the Institute as an insensitive and uncompromising manipulator, then I think you're going to have real problems down here. I don't want to do that, but I am not going to write a bunch of PR crap just to satisfy Farrow or my editor."

"Is that how you see him—a manipulator?" asked Matthews.

"Well, yes and no, from what I've seen so far. But I want to know just what you two think of the guy."

"Look, Bob," Matthews continued, "I'm not jumping on the bandwagon for Farrow, but I think he does a damn good job with what he's up against. And he's not just a pencil-pusher. He really takes an interest in what's going on and makes sure we all know where we stand on things."

"What if I told you I don't think you do?"

"What do you mean?" Matthews's demeanor and tone suggested a slight annoyance with Hendrick.

"Well, it's very nebulous at this point, but I get the distinct impression that Farrow is sitting on something—maybe a project, or anonymous funds, or . . . hell, I don't know—but something important. And *nobody's* talking about it."

Matthews shook his head, "I don't think so. I don't know of any project running that is that secretive, and I've been here four years—I think I'd know."

Hendrick couldn't decide but thought to himself, that Matthews was either telling the truth or, if lying, was a hell of a good actor. Hendrick continued, "I still think there are things that only he knows and can use—like the power play with the Senate committee he described tonight at supper. I know the way the capital boys work, and I can't believe the head of a research institute would have enough clout to call off the Governor's cronies unless he knew something."

Matthews smiled and said, "Well, I do know the answer to that one, but I'm not sure I ought to tell you."

"Why not? It's off the record."

"Well, okay. I'll just say that one of the senators had something going that would endanger his re-election and in fact would probably force him out of the political arena entirely. I don't know which one, but someone told Farrow that lease-purchase options on the northern half of the island had been filed with the Secretary of State by a holding company called Investment Properties, Inc. If for any reason the Institute went under, the property of the Institute would be available, and Investment Properties would exercise those options. Of course, the corporation was run by a front man, but who do you think owns Investment Properties?"

"The Senator?"

"You got it. And so did Farrow when he checked the records at the Secretary of State's office. Also, Farrow discovered that the other two Senators were silent partners in the corporation. It's all legal, of course, but certainly not ethical—particularly, if the Senator's the one to shut down the Institute. If that happened, then it could be criminal. Farrow called the Senator personally and thanked him for his visit to the island and for his 'obvious' interest in its welfare. I think the way he put it . . . he said that he was glad that someone of the Senator's stature served on the committee to evaluate the project, because he knew of at

81

least one member of the group who had a lot to gain by the closing of the Institute. He even mentioned the name of the holding company to the Senator. Strangely, the committee delayed their report, and action on it was shelved until a later date."

"Farrow is like that. He'll play politics with the best of them," admitted Borden. "Personally, I don't really like the man, but professionally, I agree with Walt that he runs the Institute well. I worked at the other research station on Johnson Island a year ago, and the whole operation there was screwed up. I mean, just stupid things happened. When I was there, I ran tests on protozoa and bacterial growth and had one week left to finish observations and write-ups on the separate tanks. The H.I. there arbitrarily decided nothing could be gained from my project, and he scratched the tests. The entire summer's work was aborted, and you know why? I finally got him to admit that he had to round up twenty-five more tanks for one of the university resident's experiments."

"That's right," added Matthews. "I know that's true. That kind of thing just doesn't happen here. Once you get a commitment from Farrow, he'll get you what you need, and he expects the same kind of commitment and support from you. That's why I like it here—it's tighter and everybody has a chunk of the responsibility. For example, we all know that Glen is doing phytoplankton studies and that I'm into estuarine food chains and food pyramids. We all share related material."

"I've never heard of 'phytoplankton.' What's that all about?" Borden spoke up, "Well, the easy answer to that is they are microscopic plants that are a part of aquatic food chains or webs—like Walt is working on."

"What about Stassen? Do either of you know what he was doing?"

Borden answered, "Not specifically. He did lectures, but he never described in detail his own work."

"How well did he fit into this communal picture? I got the impression he didn't."

Borden remained silent, but Matthews continued.

"Well, Stassen had other things going. I don't mean experiments. I mean things in his personal life that affected how he dealt with people. At first, I think most of us resented the fact that he was secretive about his work, but we all took into account who he was. He was the one big name that helped prevent the abandonment of the project here, and I think Farrow allowed him certain privileges because of that."

"What kind of privileges?"

"Oh, nothing out of line. Just separate living quarters—the cottage across the courtyard—and the only securable enclosed test station in the lab."

"Which Stassen kept locked?"

"I think so—at least most of the time."

"Isn't that unusual in a research community?"

"Maybe, but one of his fields of expertise was environmental spills and the effects on invertebrates—shrimps and crabs. In his lab area, he dealt with highly toxic substances. The accidental spilling of materials there could easily contaminate the artificial environment and destroy his experiments."

"Is it possible that he was conning everyone—that he had other things going?"

For the first time, both men looked at him suspiciously. Hendrick decided to soften his accusation. "Look, I'm just asking—just trying to get a clear picture of the man."

Borden answered before Matthews, "Who knows? For that matter, I could easily be doing secretive work, but it couldn't be anything major and get past Farrow."

Matthews added, "We post a running list of experiments and developments on the charts near the mailboxes so that all of us can check for project interrelationships and cross-reference data. Also, we have weekly lectures by resident staff, and at those meetings, all of us are prepared to bring everyone up-to-date on where we are in our individual areas."

"Did Stassen lecture often?"

"Only occasionally, maybe once or twice a month," answered Borden. "But when he did, it was to a packed house. Everyone knew that Stassen was tops in his field, and to have him lecturing and not attend was just stupid. He was really something to watch. After he finished an explanation and asked for questions, he seemed to open up more than he ever would on an individual basis. He was like a performer in those sessions, leading us on with bits and pieces of information rather than immediate answers. Every other sentence would begin with 'Now, why do you suppose . . . ?' He made it seem that we all were trying to solve a problem or reach a conclusion as a team. It was a helluva lot more interesting than being spoon-fed chunks of data. But then, you could ask him about something privately and he would clam up . . ." Borden quickly recognized his own joke, ". . . uh, pardon the pun." Hendrick and Matthews groaned.

"Well, he set me straight about his reticence to discuss with individuals what he had just presented in lecture or would at another time." Matthews quoted Stassen in an inept heavy German accent, "Der ees too mahch knowledge to be learned to vayste on a one-to-one basees. You breeng up deese question at my next lecture, undt I vill happily discuss it so dat all may benefit."

The three laughed at Matthews's impression.

Borden continued, "I guess the only two people who broke that barrier were Farrow and Margaret Courtney."

"Do you think Stassen had anything going there?"

"With Margaret? No. They worked closely together, I suppose, but even she couldn't get past the privacy he seemed to demand. I remember coming into the lab early one morning and saw her standing with him in his office. He was livid that she had read something on his desk, and he was really chewing her out."

Hendrick's interest heightened. "What did he say to her? Do you remember?"

"Sure . . . verbatim. He was yelling at her about his notebook. I heard him tell her, 'This notebook is my personal work—my private notes—and no one . . . *no one* has the right to them unless I say so. Is that clear?' Margaret left the office in tears, and later, after she had settled down, she told me that she had put something on his desk and found the notebook open. She read something that interested her and made the mistake of asking about it."

"Did she say what she had read?"

"Yes, but it was nothing that unusual. She couldn't understand why he became so upset. He later apologized to her and tried to explain his irritation. He told her that occasionally he got very depressed and misinterpreted people's actions. I think that they were closer after that. Margaret even got him to talk about his family whom he never discussed with anyone. Most of us thought it strange that he never left on holidays or took any time off to be with his family. As far as we knew, no one ever came to see him."

"No Mrs. Stassen?"

"I'm sure he had been married once. Somebody asked, and all he said was 'She's dead,' and walked away."

"Were there many of these confrontations or arguments with other members of the staff?"

"No. As a matter of fact, I think he kind of mellowed in the last few months. He didn't snap at anyone—just stayed to himself much more. There were periods of four and five days that he didn't come to the dining hall for meals. He had his own kitchen, and maybe he didn't like the food."

"Either of you have any ideas about his death? Do you really think it was accidental drowning?"

Hendrick thought that both men seemed surprised by the question, and they looked at each other momentarily. He watched both them intently but could not decide if their reaction revealed that they knew more than they were telling or if they simply had not given it any thought.

Matthews spoke first. "You mean suicide?"

"That. Or murder."

"*Murder*? On this island?" Borden responded. "We occasionally get on each other's nerves here, but this is a research institute, not a cloistered setting for an Agatha Christie novel."

"Look. I'm only asking. Is it possible the man either killed himself or was murdered?"

"Hell, Hendrick. Anything's possible. No one *really* knows what's on somebody's mind, and I guess he could've done himself in. But I can't accept the idea of murder—not here. I can't imagine a *motive*."

"What about visitors to the island—maybe someone outside the Institute?"

"I can't believe that either," Matthews answered.

"You know yourself that anyone coming on the island—particularly to the Institute—must have permission and declare a reason for coming. Besides, Stassen made it very clear that he did not have time to conduct tours or even talk with outside people. So Farrow just detoured visitors, even important people, around him. And he told me to do the same whenever I took guests through the Institute."

Borden interrupted, "He met somebody a week or so before he died."

"How do you know that?" Matthews asked.

"I was at the dock the night he took a boat out."

"You saw him?" Hendrick asked.

"Yeah. I had gone out walking and decided to jog down to the dock and back. He had just pulled away from the dock as I got to it, but when I asked who was taking the runabout, Curtis, the dockhand, told me Stassen had to meet someone on a yacht anchored out in the river."

Hendricks asked Borden, "Did you see it?"

"Sure. It was a little dark, but I could still see that it was big—a forty- or fifty-foot cruiser."

"Did Stassen ever say what it was about?"

"Stassen? Are you serious? No way! And you can bet your last dollar that nobody asked."

"Well," Hendrick added, "I'd sure like to know the reason for that little visit."

"How about another beer, Bob? Glen?"

"No, no thanks," Hendrick answered.

Borden stood. "Me either. As a matter of fact, I'm turning in. I've got to go to the mainland early tomorrow morning to help load some equipment that's in. See you sometime tomorrow, Walt. Nice talking to you, Bob."

"Same here." Hendrick excused himself as well and the informal get-together ended. Back in his room, he began to sort out the evening's conversation to retain what he considered important elements. While he had not concluded that Stassen's death was murder, it was becoming clear to him that the events surrounding the death were unusual, and he resolved not to leave the island without answers. From his jacket, he took his notepad and quickly jotted down the conversations, impressions, and events that might prove valuable later. He then began a list of the Institute members and included biographical data as well as related anecdotes that could provide human interest angles for his articles. Still, nagging questions concerning all of the people on his list persisted. Hendrick went over them repeatedly in his mind as he prepared for bed.

He took a quick shower and, back in his room, lay awake in the darkness for a long while. A cool, fragrant breeze softly fluttered the window blinds, and a gentle rain soon followed. He was tired, and any hope of staying awake much longer gave way to the lulling wind, the rain falling through the pines, and the constant sound of the distant surf. He was unaware of the figure outside his room and the white, sealed envelope silently sliding underneath his door.

CHAPTER 5

Hendrick awakened early in the morning. The last few moments of darkness before early morning light, filtered by the blinds, spilled into the room. Several minutes passed before he noticed the envelope on the floor by the door. He was sitting on the bed to tie his shoes when he first saw it. His first thought was that perhaps Dr. Farrow had sent someone to deliver a message and that he had not found him there. Perhaps he had even overlooked it when he came in the night before. Tearing the envelope open, he read the cryptic typewritten message:

"ASK MURDOCK ABOUT STASSEN'S DEATH. THEN MEET ME AT THE GOLDEN ANCHOR SEAFOOD HOUSE. 1:00 P.M. TODAY."

"Well, now we're getting someplace," Hendrick thought to himself. Somewhere, he had seen the name "Murdock,"

but he could not remember just where. As he walked to the cafeteria for breakfast, he tried to decide on a plan—a way to draw the anonymous writer of the note out into the open. At breakfast, Hendrick nonchalantly dropped Murdock's name, and one of the men at the table mentioned that Murdock ran a funeral home in Hagers Point. Hendrick ate and proceeded to the Administration building to get his mail and from there telephoned the mainland.

"Good morning. Murdock Funeral Home," a woman's voice answered.

"Yes ma'am. My name is Robert Hendrick of the Charleston *Courier,* and I need some information on the Stassen service a week or so ago. Did you people handle the funeral arrangements?"

"Yes, we did, Mr. Hendrick."

"Could you tell me who asked you to provide the service? I understood he had no living relatives."

"That is true. But you see, Mr. Murdock is also our elected county coroner, so we were called when Dr. Stassen was found. In a case like this, we are asked by the county to provide for funeral services if there are to be any."

"I see. Does Mr. Murdock maintain a separate office as coroner?"

"Oh no. He has all the records here at the funeral home and does his work here. It's much simpler than using two offices."

"Fine. I wonder if I might speak with him?"

"I'm sorry. He isn't here just now. Perhaps he could return your call when he gets back?"

"Actually, I'm calling from Jaheewah Island, but I've decided to come into town this morning. I can stop in, if you'll tell him to expect me."

"Certainly. He will be here all day today, but we do have a funeral this afternoon. When he gets back, I'll tell him you called, and he'll be looking for you."

"Good. I'll be in around ten."

"Do you have our address?"

"Yes, I do. And thanks for your help."

"You're welcome. Goodbye, Mr. Hendrick."

"Goodbye."

"*So,*" Hendrick conjectured, "*Whoever supplied me with Murdock's name is sending me to the man responsible for determining cause of death. No doubt the note's author will also be at the Golden Anchor at one o'clock.*"

Outside the building, Hendrick spotted Jason looking at a rusted downspout at the side of the small porch.

"Say, Jason," Hendrick called. "What time does the ferry head back to Hagers Point?"

"Eight-forty," Jason answered. "That'll put you in Hagers Point about nine-fifteen. If you're ready to go now, I'll run you down to the dock. Otherwise, you got yourself a long walk in a short time."

"Thanks. I just need to get my jacket. Be right back."

Jason and Hendrick arrived at the dock to see a handful of waiting passengers whom Hendrick attempted to identify. He noted the usual maintenance types dressed in work clothes. Four children romped on the weathered benches against the fence, and three members of the Institute stood in conversation near one of the pilings. Glen Borden, the only one of the three whose name Hendrick was sure of, seemed surprised to see Hendrick, and as they made small talk, Hendrick dismissed him as the sender of the anonymous note. The other two scientists spoke politely but showed little concern about Hendrick's presence. One of the maintenance men did eye Hendrick somewhat strangely, he thought. The man seemed to be staring at him, and when Hendrick returned his gaze, the old man slowly looked away. Hendrick continued to look at him, making a mental picture of his dark green work trousers, light tan sport shirt, and old blue suit coat. An out-of-style brown hat, pushed back on his head, completed the old man's outfit. The sound of the boat's foghorn interrupted Hendrick's concentration, and all the passengers moved to the cabin. Earlier, Hendrick had pegged Margaret Courtney as the author of the mysterious note and was surprised that she was not on board. As the boat pulled away from the dock and the engines made extended conversation futile, Hendrick thought of the reasons she seemed to him a likely candidate.

The cold wind raised small whitecaps in the river channel. The boat struck the waves viciously, slicing toward the mainland, and Hendrick appreciated the warmth of the cabin and its protection from the wind and the biting spray. The engines' drone and the whistling wind were hypnotic, and he found it easy to mull over the questions nagging at him. He glanced aft toward the island, but because of a turn in the winding river, he could only see the southern tip of Jaheewah. The sun, which had risen a few hours earlier, was now burning off the thick morning fog. He could see the tip of the island clearly, and as he looked in that direction, a bright reflection appeared over the island slightly above the horizon. The pinpoint of light intensified then disappeared.

"Did you see that?" Hendrick asked the old man sitting across the aisle. The man looked in the direction Hendrick had indicated.

"A light—I thought I saw a bright flash."

"I didn't see nothin', mister," the man replied.

For a few moments longer, Hendrick stared into the haze, waiting for whatever he had seen to reappear. After a while, he dismissed the mysterious phenomenon and began to collect his thoughts for the meeting with Murdock. By asking around, he had learned that Murdock had served as coroner for the past three terms. The few people Hendrick talked with that morning considered Charles

Murdock an honest, hard-working, civic-minded member of the community. The Murdock Funeral Home, in the family for three generations, was the "established" funeral home for the area and, according to their ad, offered the most comprehensive services available in the southeast. The Yellow Pages advertisement in the telephone directory depicted a typical two-story, wood-frame Victorian structure with large porches surrounding both floors of the house. An abundance of bentwood rocking chairs painted the same color as the trim of the old house graced the lower porch. The balustrades of the porches created ornate gingerbread designs in the negative spaces, and four dormer windows interrupted a steep, tiled roof. Through the windows, it was later suggested to Hendrick, the spirits of the dead peered out to see who was coming to pay last respects to them. Hendrick recalled a recent piece he had done on South Carolina antebellum homes—"monuments to the old south," he had called them. A blast of the foghorn drew his attention outside. Hendrick recognized the dock area where he had first met the boat. In just minutes, the boat completed a starboard turn, reversing its original direction. Maneuvering slowly against the current, the captain expertly allowed the boat to drift lightly against the pier to be moored. Having no luggage or parcels, Hendrick quickly stepped off the vessel. The dock lay at the foot of Cromwell Street just three blocks east of Hagers Point's main business area. A quiet little seacoast town, Hagers Point still boasted of old live-oak trees guarding city streets and boulevards. Near the dock area, a few rustic buildings housed small seafood restaurants and bars catering to both "locals" and tourists. Hendrick entered one of the more populated of the restaurants and took a seat at the counter.

"What'll it be, neighbor?"

"Just coffee—and some information."

The deeply tanned man, dressed in slacks and a white dress shirt open at the collar, placed a mug of steaming coffee and a spoon in front of Hendrick.

"We got plenty of coffee—I don't know about information. Cream or sugar?"

"No, I'll just have it black." Hendrick sipped the welcome hot liquid. "

"Can you tell me where the 'Golden Anchor' is?"

"Sure. It's on the other side of town out on Canton Boulevard. Just take Cromwell here on through town as far as you can, then take a left. That'll be Canton Boulevard. The 'Anchor' is a small place about three miles on out Canton on the right. You got a car?"

"No, I haven't. But I have to go to Murdock Funeral Home first, anyway. That's not far, is it?"

"No. Four blocks. On the corner of First and Cromwell."

"Great. I can walk that easy enough."

"Sure," the waiter said, grinning. "You look healthy enough to me."

"Thanks," Hendrick replied.

Refilling Hendrick's cup with fresh coffee, he continued, "Fred's the name. If you need anything else, just holler."

He turned and went to chat with another customer. The clientele, it seemed to Hendrick, were as much a part of the character of the place as any of the fixtures.

"How about a quarter for some music, mister?"

Hendrick turned to the woman who had just taken the seat beside him. He had never seen a more unkempt person. Her dirty, uncombed gray hair fell haphazardly over thick plastic-rimmed glasses. Her dress and sweater could easily have been slept in, and dark hose were tightly rolled just below knobby knees. Hendrick said nothing but gave her the coin. The blast of a popular country and western number filled the small cafe, and the old woman began a jerky dance step having nothing to do with the rhythmic accents of the music. Hendrick looked at the others in the dimly lit room. They simply smiled and shook their heads in amazement at the sad woman who teetered and whirled across the floor, dancing before tables and imaginary people. Hendrick took note of the sign taped to the mirror across from him which read: "Coffee—Always 50 cents!" Glancing at his watch, he quickly finished the coffee, placed three dollars on the counter. Hendrick got Fred's attention and asked him to give the old woman a piece of the chocolate pie from the glass-covered dish on the counter. Hendrick left the cafe, squinting momentarily as he stepped out into the bright sunlight. It was after nine-thirty, so he began walking to the funeral home.

The three blocks up to Broad Street contained most of the downtown shops and offices of Hagers Point. The storefronts had obviously undergone recent remodeling; the upper stories had either been painted or had been out-fitted with shutters to match the lower level. Hendrick was reminded of the collective renovation of downtown Carroway, South Carolina, where a cooperative move by all the businessmen to offset the shopping center chain stores had apparently been successful. On this morning, the stores seemed to have a respectable number of customers. He liked the looks of Hagers Point, South Carolina and could easily imagine himself living here—possibly editing the local paper.

At nearly ten o'clock, he hurriedly walked the remaining block to the funeral home. The stately old house and the landscaping immediately caught his eye. Flowering shrubs and bushes softened the lower porch line, and beautifully kept grass inched against the winding walkways and stairs leading to the entrance to the house. Smaller shrubs flanked the wooden "Murdock Funeral Home" sign, set in the same bricks that bordered the stone walkways to the front of the house. Hendrick stepped onto the porch and opened one of the double front doors. They contained large glass sections etched in an ornate floral design and a graceful initial "M." An attractive middle-aged woman at the desk looked up and in a quiet voice greeted him.

"May we help you, sir?"

The woman, dressed in a subdued brown and white print dress, sat behind a distinctive and highly polished mahogany desk. On the wide desktop sat a telephone and a large lamp, which provided the only light in the hallway. Brochures and an appointment book lay neatly before her, and to her left sat a vase of delicately arranged, freshly cut flowers. Four large parlors for visitors and families of the deceased opened off the hallway which led to a wide staircase.

"Yes. I'm Robert Hendrick. I called earlier. I would like to see Mr. Murdock, if that's possible."

"Of course, Mr. Hendrick. He's expecting you." She lifted the telephone receiver to her ear and dialed two digits.

"Mr. Hendrick's here, Mr. Murdock." There was a short pause, and she said, "Yes, sir. I'll show him the way."

Hanging up, she stood, casually smoothing her dress.

"Right this way, Mr. Hendrick," she said softly.

She led him past the staircase and then stopped momentarily at an office on the right. She knocked, then opened the door for him.

"Go right in, Mr. Hendrick."

"Thank you, ma'am," he said. "Thank you very much."

"Hello there, Mr. Hendrick. Come on in— have a seat."

Murdock's booming voice seemed incongruous—almost irreverent. Murdock returned to his desk, and Hendrick sat across from him on a couch against the wall. Murdock was a stocky man—balding somewhat, handsomely tanned from hours out-doors, and dressed in a dark suit, white shirt, and dark striped tie. Murdock seemed not only aware of Hendricks's scrutiny of him but also a little amused at it. He stretched his arms downward as if to better reveal his outfit and continued. "We have a funeral this afternoon and I'm afraid this is my uniform. I'd much rather wear my golf shorts and a sport shirt, but somehow I feel the living among our clients would object." They laughed.

"Cigar?" He extended an ornately carved and brass plated box.

"No thanks. I don't smoke."

"Good for you! I'm trying to cut down myself. Tell me, how may we be of service to you? Mrs. Parsons says you were interested in the Stassen service?"

105

"I'll try to be brief. I don't know if Mrs. Parsons told you, but I'm with the Charleston *Courier*."

"Yes, I think she did mention that. Damn good paper! It's been around for a long time. I don't recall noticing your name—do you have a regular column?"

"No, I just cover various news items that come along—and occasional feature stories. Actually, I'm down here on Jaheewah Island to do some articles on the Marine Biology Institute and, of course, Dr. Stassen's contribution was particularly important. I just wanted to clarify a few things before writing about Stassen."

"What kind of things?"

"Oh . . . just the events and details of his death . . . from an official point of view. You did rule on that didn't you, Mr. Murdock?"

"Yes, oh yes. I am the coroner. Let me get the file." Murdock rose and turned to cabinets built into the wall behind him.

"I believe we ruled accidental drowning, if I'm remembering right. Yes, here it is . . . 'Dr. Heinrich E. Stassen, September 17. Cause of death: accidental drowning.' "

"That's what I wanted to ask about. When you first saw him, you were sure it was accidental drowning?"

"Actually, we made that decision on the basis of the report filed by my assistant who received the body. I didn't personally examine the body." Murdock sat again at the desk with the file before him.

"Isn't that a little unusual?"

"Not really. Let me explain how this office works, and maybe that'll help. You see, I'm responsible for this whole county, one of the largest in the state and also the islands. That's a big area, Mr. Hendrick, and while we don't have people dropping like flies, there are a significant number of deaths—ninety-nine percent of them from natural causes. Now, by statute, I'm allowed one qualified assistant who, in my absence, is authorized to file a report which, of course, I look over later to confirm and approve. He initials the report, and I sign it later if I am unable to view the corpse."

"Is that what happened in Stassen's case?"

"Exactly. I was out of town when they found him, so Mrs. Parsons sent Mike—he was my assistant at that time—over to the island to collect the body."

"*Was* your assistant?"

"That's right. He left for the fall term at med school. You see, what I try to do is give some young medical student a chance to work with me rather than hire some flunky off the street. Mike's a sharp boy—very thorough in every report he wrote up for me. He was an honor student his last semester at school with straight A's in his courses. I never had any questions about his work."

"So, actually, he filed the report."

"That's right. Under my signature, of course."

"May I see the report?"

Murdock looked quizzically at Hendrick then smiled broadly. "Certainly. These are public records."

Hendrick read the form quickly but carefully. "I see 'M.H.' initialed here—above your signature. I assume those are your assistant's initials?"

"That's right. 'Halston' is Mike's last name. Then I signed it there to acknowledge that I had okayed the report and concurred with the established cause of death."

"Accidental drowning?"

"That's correct."

"How can you be sure it was accidental—that it wasn't criminal—without seeing the body?"

"*Criminal*?" Murdock's expression betrayed his visible discomfort. He seemed to become more guarded in his comments, Hendrick judged. "Are you saying that you think Stassen was murdered?"

"Let's just say I am curious about his death, and I'd like to know exactly how the man died. That's all."

"Well, I don't believe anything in that report suggests murder. Mike told me that he could find no evidence of foul play—no bruises, no cuts, no contusions—so that's why he wrote 'Cause of death: probable accidental drowning.' Had I been there, I would've reached the same conclusion."

"Then there was no autopsy?"

"Nope. Nobody asked for one. We had the hearing, and we were authorized to arrange for cremation of the body and did so."

"And you don't know if he had water in the lungs or not. Could he have had a heart attack?"

"He could have, I guess, but I don't think it makes much difference now. He was cremated, you know. I don't really see what you're after, Mr. Hendrick." Murdock was becoming more irritated and his face reddened noticeably.

"Look. I don't intend to suggest any culpability on your part. I'm just concerned that I not overlook anything having to do with Stassen's death."

"Let's just lay the cards on the table, Mr. Hendrick. You are implying by your questions a lack of integrity on my part to represent the best intentions and responsibilities of the county coroner's office, and *I feel* that we've handled this situation in a proper and professional manner."

"Not at all, Mr. Murdock. I'm not down here to criticize in any way you or your work as coroner. I'm just asking for your help in explaining Stassen's death. There's one thing that makes me certain now that whatever happened to him out there, he did not drown. And it's right here in this report, which I assume you at least read before you signed."

"*Really!* Can you show me what leads you to that conclusion? How do you know the man didn't drown?"

"Lividity, Mr. Murdock." Hendrick rose and came to the side of the desk, then read aloud from the report: " . . . 'lividity located in the small of the back and the backs of the legs.' Now if I understand lividity—it takes the blood once it has stopped flowing 30-60 minutes to collect and form the dark color in the body—in the lowest level once it is in a prone position. I'm sure you know that in the water, the weight of the arms and legs causes a corpse to float face down. If somebody drowned, there would be discoloration in the chest and abdomen as well as in the calves— but not along the back. And there would be water in the lungs. Stassen may very well have had a heart attack and lay on his back a couple of hours before the tide washed him out, but he sure as hell didn't drown.

Murdock looked stunned. Hendrick watched him intently. He could not decide what Murdock's hesitation meant but then realized that Murdock had either completely overlooked the lividity findings or perhaps had not even read the report before he signed it. Finally, Murdock looked up from the paper and spoke less aggressively.

"You might be right on this, Hendrick, but I really don't see that it makes much difference now. What do you want to do?"

"To start, I'd like a copy of that report."

"Are you going to be in town for a while?"

"I've got an appointment at one o'clock, and I have to catch the boat back to the island at five."

"I tell you what. Why don't you stop by on your way to the ferry, and we'll have the copy for you. Our copier is down, but Mrs. Parsons will be going to the bank before then, and she can make copies over there. Naturally, for legal reasons, I can't just give you the original report."

"That's fine. I appreciate your cooperation.

"Thank you, Mr. Hendrick. Now, if you'll excuse me, I have to check on arrangements for this afternoon's funeral."

"Certainly. I'll find my own way out."

Both men stood, shook hands, and Hendrick retraced his steps into the hallway. Mrs. Parsons looked up and smiled as he approached.

"Good day, sir."

"The same to you, ma'am. By the way, could you tell me where I might catch a taxi?"

"Usually, one is parked on Broad Street just down that way a block. But I'd be happy to call a cab for you, if you like."

"No, no thanks," Hendrick replied, glancing at his watch. "I don't need it just yet. I'll just walk around town a bit. So long."

"Goodbye, Mr. Hendrick. Enjoy your stay."

Nearly an hour later, Hendrick had tired of his walk down several side streets, around a courthouse square, and finally to the corner of Broad and Cromwell. There sat a dilapidated 1958 black and white Chevy with "TAXI" lettered on the sides, the trunk, and on the small, lighted fixture on the car's roof. Hendrick looked around for the driver then leaned against the door on the passenger side of the car to wait. Presently, a tall, black man emerged from the corner drugstore and approached Hendrick.

"Where to, mister?"

"The Golden Anchor—out on Canton Boulevard, I believe."

"That's right. Hop in, an' I'll take you right to the place."

The man opened Hendrick's door then went around to the driver's side. He turned the key in the ignition, and the starter ground away for several seconds before the engine roared to life. With the scraping sound of meshing gears, they turned onto Cromwell Street and sped out the thoroughfare in front of a curtain of blue-black smoke.

"I suppose you got a good reason for going way out here to eat your dinner?"

"Why? Isn't the food good?"

"Sure enough! It's probably better than any place in town, but most of the tourists want something a little nicer. Use to be, all the fancy places was out here overlooking the marshes. They cleaned up the docks on the other side of town; then everything done moved down there. The Anchor's the only one that's stayed open out here. There sure won't be many people there this time of day."

As they reached the intersection and turned left onto Canton, Hendrick observed old boathouses, other abandoned buildings, and vacant lots.

"They's gonna make a park out here so people can look out on the marshes. They're supposed to try to clean up the water so people can swim an' run their boats up an' down the river."

"I see. It ought to be real nice."

"Yessir. You gonna need a ride back into town?"

"I don't know yet. I'm meeting someone who can probably give me a lift into town."

"Well, if you do need a ride, just call for the Black and White cab. We're in the phone book. Just ask for 'Jimmie,' an' I'll be glad to come get you."

"Thanks, Jimmie. I'll remember, and thanks for the tour."

Most of the buildings had been torn down, and at the gravel turnoff into a parking lot, the Golden Anchor appeared rather forlorn standing by itself along the treeless bank of the waterway. Jimmie pulled in and, after being paid, sped away leaving Hendrick on the gravel lot in a cloud of exhaust.

Hendrick turned to face the rustic façade of the old restaurant. On the roof of the board-and-batten building rested a large wooden sign: "Golden Anchor." Hendrick conjectured, "Golden" had apparently been added later to "modernize."

The front of the building, bleached by hot sun, stood windowless but with double heavy wooden doors. Hendrick noticed only a single car in the parking lot. Glancing at his watch, he saw that he had arrived at exactly one o'clock. Except for the one car, the place looked closed. Opening the heavy door, he waited a few seconds for his eyes to adjust to the darkness of the foyer. *"What a perfect place for a clandestine meeting,"* he thought. Old fixtures, adapted from various kinds of nautical gear, softly lit the interior. High-backed booths were arranged along the side walls, and at each, an old ship's porthole admitted the only daylight. Once settled into a booth, a couple could almost be invisible.

A young lady approached him and asked, "May I show you to a seat, sir?"

"Thanks. I'm supposed to meet someone, but I don't see anybody I know."

"No, sir. You're our only customer right now."

"I'll just have some tea while I wait."

"That's just fine. Hot or cold? Sweet or unsweet?"

"Oh . . . iced tea, please . . . unsweetened."

The waitress showed him to a booth, and he sat facing the doorway. She had just brought his tea when a shaft of bright sunlight spilled into the dark foyer. Hendrick watched the creaking door with increasing curiosity. A tall man entered—no one Hendrick recognized. The man spoke briefly to the waitress and took a seat at one of the tables in the center of the room.

In a few minutes, the door opened again, and a well-dressed young woman appeared. At first Hendrick did not recognize her, but as the light from the closing door faded and she turned toward him, he saw her face clearly. Margaret Courtney looked quite different to him in this setting than she did working in the lab, where she usually wore faded jeans and a sweatshirt.

117

JAHEEWAH

CHAPTER 6

Margaret Courtney glanced around the dimly lit room and, after spotting Hendrick, motioned to the waitress that she would join him. As she approached, Hendrick rose to greet her.

"Hello, Margaret. I thought we might be having lunch together, but when you weren't on the boat, I wasn't sure."

She slid into the booth, and he sat across from her. Strangely, she seemed more mature, more attractive than the young girl he had met on the island. She wore tan slacks and light brown suede jacket over a colorful print blouse. Her dark brown hair seemed longer than he remembered, and it glistened in the sunlight from the window.

"I came over last night and stayed with a friend." She glanced around and continued, "I know this isn't very classy, but it's private—and they still have the best shrimp in town. Do you mind meeting here?"

"Of course not." He looked at her and smiled. "As a matter of fact, though this is somewhat unexpected, I've been looking forward to spending some unofficial time with you." She first looked away then returned his smile. The waitress arrived to take their order, and they both chose a shrimp dinner. Over cocktails and the meal, they talked casually and occasionally laughed at each other's anecdotes.

Over coffee, Hendrick changed the subject. "Well, Margaret, I know what brings me here for this intimate meeting, but I'm very curious about why you're here."

"I'm not sure myself. Except that I began to see in you someone to help me figure some things out, and I wondered if you would."

"Things about Stassen's death, I take it?"

She looked up from her coffee cup, the rim of which she had been circling with her index finger. "Yes."

"What about it?"

"What if I told you that I don't believe for a minute Dr. Stassen died accidentally?"

Hendrick coyly smiled. "What if I told you that I don't believe it was an accident or suicide either, for that matter?"

"You don't?"

"No. I'm almost sure of it. But why the anonymous note? Didn't you talk to someone about it?"

"Who? How could I know for sure that whomever I talked to was not the one responsible for his death? Before we continue, I need your assurance of confidentiality. Besides, even if there was nothing to it, I could still lose my position on the island because of the publicity. When you came and we talked, I thought that you would be uninvolved and objective—free from pressure to keep quiet. But I didn't know you, and I didn't know if I could trust you. I also know that I am taking a chance talking with you about this whole thing."

"So, what you're saying is . . . you think Stassen was murdered, and you want some help."

"Exactly," she nodded her head. "Because I knew Stassen was too careful to drown. He thoroughly understood wetland environments and was well aware of tidal flow and seaward currents."

"What about suicide?"

"No. He had access to any number of more efficient ways to kill himself."

"Look, Margaret. You're in a serious area when you start talking murder, and I think you do need some help. But I'm thinking the same thing, and I intend to get some answers. I don't want to involve you more than I have to, but I'd like to hear everything you can tell me. And if you're still frightened and don't want anyone to know about this conversation, that's okay by me. But I have to trust you in what you're telling me, and you've got to trust me enough to tell me everything you know or think you know. Okay?"

"Okay."

"First of all, I don't see you as a suspect . . . you didn't kill him, did you?"

"Bob!" she answered in mock disgust.

"Let's begin with your message. How did you know about Murdock?"

"Well, I didn't really know anything except that he actually didn't come to get Dr. Stassen's body. A young guy from the funeral home did, and he was making notes on a form of some kind."

"Was it just notes?"

"Yes. I think so. I was really upset about what might happen to Stassen's body. The guy said that Murdock had been called out of town and told me that he would take the body back to the funeral home to complete a forensic examination. I found out later that Murdock, as coroner, would have to rule on the death, and I couldn't understand how this kid could legally be doing the pathology. I knew that I couldn't go to Murdock myself without telling Dr. Farrow. I just felt like he would consider it inappropriate. It probably would have been. I thought Murdock would have to tell a reporter more than he would have to tell me, so I sent you the note hoping you would talk to him."

"I did—less than an hour ago."

"Really? What did he say?"

"Enough to let me know that he probably didn't even read the pathology report. The guy you saw was a 'Mike Halston,' Murdock's assistant. I think he not only transferred the body to the funeral home, but probably also wrote the coroner's report. He initialed the forms and left them for Murdock to approve and sign. I'm supposed to go back there later this afternoon for a photocopy. From what I read, I know he didn't drown, but I haven't been able to figure out how he did die. Do you have any idea who might benefit from his death—someone who might like to see him dead?"

"No. He was known all over the world and I guess had quite a bit of money. He told me once that he had set up trusts naming several institutes as beneficiaries. I understood that he had no family left."

"I've gotten the impression that he was very secretive about his work—even with you."

"That's right. Officially, I was his lab assistant, but I spent most of the time working on my own stuff. Most things I did for him were menial—like cleaning beakers and tanks. There were a few tests he allowed me to monitor. At first, it worried me, and I asked several times if he wanted me to help with some of his main experiments and tests, but he always found something else for me to do."

"I understand that once he even chewed you out about his notebook or something."

She seemed surprised. "How did you know about that?"

Hendrick grinned, "I'm a reporter, Margaret. Glen Borden told me. What was it all about?"

"Well, I noticed his notebook open on the desk and read something in it. He always kept it put away. I thought it would be fascinating to read all of his notes. His entries were beautifully detailed and thorough. When I asked him, he hit the ceiling. He surprised me, because it seemed so unlike him to lash out like that."

"Was what you read so important?"

"No. I forget now—but it was just some preliminaries and didn't mean much out of context."

"Maybe he was afraid of what you would find if you read all of his notes."

"Maybe."

"You didn't read over his notes after he died?"

"No. I was so upset that I didn't think of it until a few days after his death. By then, the notebook was gone."

"You don't know who has it?"

Her expression quickly changed. "*Yes!*" She said excitedly. "Yes, I do. I hadn't until just now but I know exactly who has it. Dr. Farrow. I don't know why I didn't think of it before."

"Did you see him take it?"

"Yes. You see, the day after they found Dr. Stassen, I came into the lab earlier than I normally do and met Dr. Farrow as he was leaving Stassen's office. When he saw me, he said that, because of Stassen's death I had been reassigned to Dr. Morrison, one of the other teaching research staff. I asked if I might continue with any of Stassen's tests and he said, 'Of course not. Dr. Holtzman has been given that assignment and has his own assistant'. So, that moved me out of that lab and into the one I'm in now. I was so upset about the transfer I didn't notice it at the time, but I distinctly remember now his having the notebook under his arm. I went back a few days later and discovered that all of Stassen's tests in the shrimp tanks had been discontinued. I simply could not believe it. I mean, Dr. Stassen had years of research behind some of those tests, and someone with the notebook could easily continue Stassen's work. When I complained to Dr. Morrison about it, he agreed and promised to discuss it at a staff meeting. He didn't say any more about it, and when I pressed him for justification, he said that he and the two other senior residents had confronted Farrow about it. According to him, Farrow convinced them all that there was no further need to continue the tests—Stassen's test results had been satisfactorily concluded and, in their view, need not be made immediately available."

"So with the experiments aborted and the notebook missing or even destroyed, there's no official or accurate record of what Stassen was doing?"

"That's right."

"And you're sure Farrow has the notebook?"

"Yes. I just don't know if he still has it."

"I think we have to find that notebook. Has anyone besides Farrow acted strangely since Stassen's death?"

"I don't know. I imagine to some people I've acted strangely, but that doesn't mean I killed Dr. Stassen."

127

"Were there other things that made you suspicious?"

"It's all kind of mixed up in my mind. I mean, it seemed to me that immediately after Stassen was found, a feeling of tension came over the whole island—even in people who supposedly had not had that much direct contact with Stassen or the Institute."

"Can you give me an example?"

"Well . . . do you know who Beebo is?"

"Yes. Jason introduced me to him the first day I was here."

"A day or two after Dr. Stassen was found, a group of workmen were taking a lunch break by the side of the maintenance barn. They were talking about Dr. Stassen when Beebo walked up. Sometimes they tease the old guy, and when he said, 'Jaheewah got him—got Stassen,' that's all they needed. They kept saying that he didn't know what he was talking about and that there was never any old bird big enough to haul off a man. Beebo got excited, and said that he had seen Jaheewah—had seen him do it. Then, apparently, they scared Beebo and he ran away. I realize that Beebo is superstitious, but something must have happened to make him think of the legend. And also, Farrow blew his

128

top about their teasing Beebo. He said that he would fire, on the spot, anybody who even mentioned Stassen or Ja- heewah to Beebo again. I could understand being mad about it, but Jason told me that Dr. Farrow called the en- tire maintenance crew in and threatened to fire all of them if anything like that happened again."

"So you think Farrow overreacted?"

"Seems so to me."

"What about Farrow's and Stassen's relationship?"

"That's hard to say because recently there seemed to be very little contact between them. I don't think Farrow was intimidated by Dr. Stassen though—he just seemed to stay clear of him. As a matter of fact, I think I may have inter- rupted quite an argument once. Dr. Stassen and I were alone in the lab, and when Farrow came in, he asked me to leave for a while. When I returned, Farrow was still fuming about something, and Stassen was also irate."

"When was that?"

"I think about a week before he died."

"Did they have any other arguments?"

"Not that I know of. After that, Dr. Stassen quit coming to the dining hall. I guess they wanted to avoid each other."

"What about meals? He had to eat."

"I assume he ate in his cottage."

"Have you ever been there?"

"No. And that's another strange thing. Dr. Farrow had the cottage locked up tight. As far as I know, no one has gone in since."

"What about Stassen's personal belongings?"

"I don't know."

"From what you say, Farrow seems awfully anxious to prevent any investigation of Stassen. You're sure about the cottage—that Farrow himself had it locked?"

"Of course. He's the H.I. No one else would have the authority."

"Let me ask you something else. What kind of guy was Stassen? What was he to you?"

"Well, as I said, he was internationally known and had written more books and articles in his field than anyone else. Naturally, I felt I had won an academy award when I found out I had been appointed to work with him. Truthfully, I guess he frightened me at first, but that quickly wore off. Very few people seemed to like Stassen, and I felt kind of sorry for him—because he seemed to be alone so much. But he could do nice things for people, and most of the time no one knew."

"Really? Like what?" Hendrick's interest heightened. He wanted to know the man. He wanted to know why someone might kill such an eminent scientist, sequestered in a cloistered, harmonious environment.

"Well . . . there's this guy—one of the maintenance men—who had done some things for Dr. Stassen, and Stassen seemed to be really grateful. I think that they once had to work through the night to prevent leaking oil from getting into his test plot. This guy had a big family, like nine or ten kids, and Stassen began providing them with some shrimp."

"What do you mean 'providing' them?"

"Actually, Dr. Stassen allowed him to take some of the live shrimp that were brought into the lab two or three times a week. The rules say that no one is to take anything from the lab, but Dr. Stassen always put four or five pounds of shrimp in a cooler. I saw him do it once, and afterwards, I saw the man walk out of the lab with the bag of shrimp. I started to report it but decided Dr. Stassen was just trying to help the guy out."

"So you didn't say anything?"

"No. And I'm glad I didn't, because soon after I became aware of Stassen's gift, one of the man's children died—a little girl. I would really have felt terrible complaining about a few pounds of shrimp."

"The child died? When was that in relation to Stassen's death?"

"About a week before, I think. Why?"

"I dunno. I just hadn't heard about another death on the island. How did she die?"

"I'm not sure . . . seems like it was a blood disease or something like that."

"Maybe it was the shrimp."

"I don't see how, because the whole family ate the same meal, and no one else got sick. Besides, I'm sure Stassen never gave the man anything but fresh shrimp."

"Who would I ask about the child's death? Is there a family physician?"

"No. Probably Dr. Palliston. He's the resident physician for the Institute and would know about them. Most of the island families go to Palliston rather than someone on the mainland."

"What else can you tell me about Stassen?"

"You mean his background?"

"Anything."

"There isn't much more I can tell you. He was German-born and immigrated from Dresden, I think. I'm not sure, but his records are on file in Dr. Farrow's office. I think this year made his third or fourth at the Institute. He had arranged to take a leave of absence next year to go to Sweden—at the University of Stockholm—for a year of lectures and more research."

"Would he return to the island after that?"

"Probably not."

"That was public knowledge?"

"Yes. Everybody I knew was aware of it."

"Can you tell me anything about his work in the lab—in layman's terms?"

"Not much. Except that he was working on preventive immunities to toxic spills from oil tankers and such. Like I said, except maybe for Farrow and the staff, no one knew exactly what tests he had running. But he concentrated on the shrimp. I could see in some of the tanks a kind of progression in the appearance of the shrimp . . . mainly in the size. They grew larger and showed an increased aggressiveness, but that's about all I could notice without access to his notes."

"Could he have been trying to develop bigger and better tasting shrimp—maybe to entice the shrimp industries?"

"I couldn't say for certain, but that kind of commercial exploitation of his work would be anathema for him. The main reason for that would be the money, and he apparently was wealthy from all his publications. His basic marine biology text is like a Bible for anyone going into the field. I'm sure that he made a very comfortable living from it alone."

The waitress reappeared with more coffee and asked if there would be anything else. Hendrick took the check and thanked the waitress.

"I guess I need to go, Margaret. When you get back to the lab, I wonder if you could do a few things for me."

"Sure. Whatever I can."

"First of all, get into Stassen's office and look for anything you can find that might have been overlooked when it was cleaned out."

"Like what? I know they emptied the desk and also the filing cabinets."

"I dunno. Just anything that might give us a clue about what he was working on. And also, see if you can find out where all his personal belongings are now. Do you feel comfortable doing that?"

"Yeah. I'll try."

"Good. Are you going back to the island?"

"I had planned to stay tonight with my friend, Heather, but I guess I could go on back."

"No. It's probably best if we go back separately. Did you drive here yourself or take a cab?"

"I have Heather's car."

"Maybe you could drop me by the funeral home."

"Sure."

After paying the check, Hendrick pushed open the heavy door, and they emerged onto the parking lot, shielding their eyes from the bright sun.

"This reminds me of when I was a kid coming out of the movie theater on Saturday mornings."

On the way back, their conversation no longer included Stassen or his mysterious death. They talked instead about the meal and their getting to know one another. Margaret stopped the car in front of Murdock's funeral home. Her hand rested on the gear shift between them, and Hendrick gently touched her arm.

"I enjoyed it, Margaret. I'll see you tomorrow on the island. When will you get there?"

"Early. I've got some things to do in the lab. Thanks for the lunch. It really should've been my treat, you know."

"That's okay. My pleasure. I'll let you know what I find out in here." Hendrick awkwardly got out of the small foreign car and waved as she drove off. He went through the double doors of the funeral home and entered the hallway.

A surprised Mrs. Parsons greeted him.

"Why, Mr. Hendrick. I didn't expect to see you again so soon."

Hendrick glance at his watch. It was nearly five o'clock.

"I came back for the copy of the coroner's report."

She look puzzled. "What report is that, Mr. Hendrick?"

"You were to have made me a copy of the coroner's report on Dr. Stassen."

"Why, I know nothing about that. Are you sure?"

"Of course. Mr. Murdock said that your copier was down and that you'd go to the bank to make a copy."

"I don't know why I'd go to the bank when our copier was printing fine just a few minutes ago."

"It's not broken?"

"Why no, sir."

"Well, maybe I had better talk with Mr. Murdock."

"But he isn't here just now, Mr. Hendrick. He had to go up to Charleston. I'd be happy to make you an appointment."

"No, that won't be necessary." Hendrick decided to soft-pedal his irritation. "Just one item Mr Murdock and I discussed interests me. Perhaps you could show me the form again."

"Well, I guess I could do that, but I know I'd better ask Mr. Murdock before I let you have Mr. Murdock's file copy."

"Of course. But I would like to see it once more before I leave for the island."

"Certainly." They walked to Murdock's office, and Mrs. Parsons pulled out the appropriate drawer. She withdrew the file marked 'Stassen', and a worried expression crossed her face. "Why, there's nothing here! The file is empty."

Hendrick saw that she was just as surprised as he and decided not to question her further about it.

"Perhaps he has it with him and intends to deliver it to you himself," she suggested.

"Perhaps. Well, I'll be going now, Mrs. Parsons. I will want to see Mr. Murdock again, but I'll call before I come in."

"That's fine, Mr. Hendrick. I certainly am sorry for the confusion. I . . . I just didn't know."

"I understand. Thank you, Mrs. Parsons."

Hendrick walked out to the street. On his way to the dock, he tried to reason out Murdock's motivation for removing the report from the file. On the boat, his thoughts revolved around unanswered questions and his pleasant lunch with Margaret Courtney. He liked her—and trusted her. He felt certain that her questions about Stassen's death and, particularly, Farrow's actions had some plausibility, and they now shared an alliance which would draw them closer together—an appealing prospect he welcomed at this point.

It had begun to shower, and Hendrick welcomed the cabin's protection from the wind and the rain. The engines roared to their cruising speed and Hendrick stared at the brown shoreline sliding by the vessel. Waterfowl and marsh rabbits were busily foraging for food, and an occasional fish leapt from the water. In the mist of the rain, the island lay before him like a gigantic sea creature floating slowly on the horizon.

CHAPTER
7

The twenty-five minute boat ride back to the island had been uneventful, and Hendrick understood more clearly why many of the regular commuters who made the trip twice daily seldom looked out the dirty windows, choosing instead to nap or read the paper. When they arrived at the island, the soft glow of the dock lights through the mist bathed the dock in warm light, highlighting the freshly painted pilings and dock house.

Jason stood leaning casually against the fence rail which bordered the dock area. Hendrick had not made arrangements to be met and was glad to see him.

"Hello, Jason. Are you waiting for somebody?"

"Yep. Doc Farrow sent me to get you. He says he wants you to pay him a little visit to his place after supper, if you wouldn't mind."

Hendrick grinned. "Well, I'll just check my social calendar and see if I can't work him in."

Jason smiled and motioned Hendrick toward the jeep.

"You know, Mr. Hendricks, if you tried a little harder you could be right funny. Get in. They's fried chicken tonight, an' I don't want to miss my share on your account."

They reached the dining hall more quickly than Hendrick expected. On the way, it occurred to Hendrick that he had told no one about his trip to the mainland—yet, somehow Farrow knew. Several of the Institute members were visiting with each other outside the dining hall, but some were still eating as Hendrick and Jason entered the building. Jason was right. The smell of fried chicken filled the room, and Hendrick found himself surprisingly hungry despite his shrimp lunch earlier. He ate quickly then excused himself to walk the few hundred yards to Farrow's cottage. A screen door was latched, but the front door itself stood open, allowing him to see a small foyer with a glow of light coming from another room off to the left. He knocked a few times and called inside.

"Hello—anybody home?"

"Yes," Farrow answered. As he came to the door, he greeted Hendrick warmly. "Come in, come in, Bob." Farrow quickly unlatched the door and grasped Hendrick's hand.

"I appreciate your coming by. Come in, and have a seat." Noticing Hendrick's obvious interest in the room, Farrow continued. "This was the guest house originally," he explained. "Some of the furnishings were left here by the Randolph family who used to own the island. Old man Randolph was quite a wheeler-dealer, so there's no telling how many agreements or ventures were planned in this very room.

"I see."

"You can have your choice, Bob. Millie's made some coffee, or I can offer you some excellent brandy."

"Coffee will be fine, thanks."

"Good. Millie?" Farrow called into the kitchen. "We'll have the coffee now." He continued to Hendrick, "Millie's been my housekeeper since we opened the Institute. She does a good job of keeping this place presentable."

"You're not married, I take it."

"No. No, my wife died about fifteen years ago—a cancer took her. So far, I haven't found anyone to take her place. And I'm afraid there hasn't been a line of independently wealthy widows willing to put up with me or my hours. You married, Bob?"

"No, sir."

"Well . . . a young man like you—there's plenty of time. Plenty of time. Ah, here's Millie."

The housekeeper, thin and gray-haired, entered slowly with a silver coffee service and various tea biscuits. She wore a simple housedress and a colorful apron. She seemed rather shy to Hendrick—never looking at him directly.

"Millie, this is Mr. Hendrick from the *Courier*. He's down here to do some stories on the Institute."

The woman carefully placed the service on the coffee table before them and smiled at Farrow. Hendrick stood and extended his hand. The woman smiled, and nodded in his direction as he stood. Only then did he realize that she was blind.

"That'll be all for tonight, Millie. You can go on home if you like. I'll clean the dishes later."

"Yessir. Good night, Dr. Farrow."

"Good night, Millie. Be careful walking home."

After she left the room and they heard the screen door shut behind her, Farrow continued, "Remarkable woman. Two years ago, her vision was perfectly normal. Then one day, she couldn't see well. It was macular degeneration—the worst stage or late AMD. In her case, the vision loss was pretty sudden. Fortunately, she had worked here and knew the place. And even now, she knows every inch of this cottage like the palm of her hand. I've had her serve refreshments to four or five guests, and none of them notices that she's practically blind. I make sure that they are all seated, and then I tell her where they are. She puts hors d'oeuvres and drinks on tables before them rather than trying to hand things around, and it works fine. It is really fascinating to watch her. She'll come in and feel for the corner of the table with her foot or leg before she leans down to place the tray. With her little fingers extended underneath, she feels for the edge of the table. She'll then slowly slide the tray onto the edge of the table, and if she feels some resistance, she'll know someone has left a glass or a plate there. Millie can identify the item just by the sound. She'll ask them to move the glass or plate for her just as if she was looking at it. If I'm having a dinner party or a lot of people over, I don't ask her to help serve. The sound and the smoke are just too much for her."

"That's really something."

"Yes, it is." Farrow paused briefly and then continued, "Well, Bob, I hope my invitation didn't sound too mysterious. I wanted to invite you personally, but Jason said that you were on the mainland."

"_So, Jason's my watchdog,_" Hendrick thought to himself. "Yes, a friend of mine had invited me to lunch and I wanted to look around Hagers Point a bit."

"Good. It's a nice town—good people. They've been real nice to us down here. You know, some of the students get awfully bored and occasionally get a little rowdy, but we haven't had the first bit of real trouble. I want to keep it that way."

"I can imagine."

"By and large, I'm proud of the Institute. We've managed to maintain a more than favorable reputation among our colleagues. And if we can keep our funding at a reasonable level, we ought to be on the way to some important research here. Forgive me, Bob. I just realized how that must sound to you. I really didn't ask you over to pump you full of propaganda."

"Not at all, Dr. Farrow. That's why I'm down here, and I do appreciate having the administrator's view of the project."

"Well, I want to be helpful in supplying you with whatever information you need, but I think I had better just let you ask the questions. I'm not very good at writing articles. I will level with you, Bob. We need your help—that is if you feel like you can give it. There are a lot of people who pull the strings on our program—from the Governor on down—and a lot of them couldn't care less about the life cycle of a crab. But I hope my staff is proving to you that there is more going on here than most people think. With the increase in housing development and destruction of habitat, the whole ecosystem of the Eastern Seaboard is in jeopardy, and it's our position that somebody had better investigate it."

"Isn't 'jeopardy' a little strong?"

"Have you ever read anything about chaos theory?"

"No, I haven't."

"It has to do with the notion that any force that causes a small change in a complex system will result in some sort of larger change in that system's surroundings. It could be as simple as someone sneezing, which causes a change in air pressure, which causes other air currents to change, and so on. And, of course, waves get started way out at sea as small waves, probably the result of storms, and they increase in intensity by the time they reach shore. This is a gross over-simplification, but what it all boils down to is balance. Tip the scales too much one way, and the whole system suffers—sometimes irrevocably. Let me give you an example. You know anything about alligators, Bob?"

"Enough to avoid them!"

"Well, they have a kind of built-in forecaster of water levels in the estuaries and surrounding marshes. It's amazing to us, but they know how high the water will get in their breeding areas almost a year in advance. Thanks to this internal predictor, they build their nests just above the normal high water level, and everything's fine. Then along comes a developer who plops down tons of fill dirt to set his houses on and this, of course, alters the water level in other areas *considerably*. The high water floods out the nests, and that whole nesting season is lost. That results in underpopulation which means overpopulation of what the alligators feed on. It's a food chain, and it's hard to read- just."

"I see. But you must admit that the average person doesn't feel the same environmental concerns you people do."

"Of course—which is why we're here. I know that we have difficulty at times communicating to the layperson the significance of what we're doing. We need someone to clearly describe and publicize what the consequences are. People, in general, just don't understand what we're up against. I'll give you another example of chaos theory: One of our students was dating a young elementary school teacher. He told her something about his experiments in phytoplankton growth. She was doing a unit on the ocean environment. These kids had never heard of an ecosystem, had never heard of plankton, and so she brought them over to see our labs. She even had a photographer come with her, and a very nice article showing the kids doing some of the tests themselves appeared in the paper. They went back and set up a miniature ecosystem in their room.

149

It was great to see the level of their interest. That experience and the article were some of the best PR we could hope for. This is why we've asked you down here. Your editor convinced me that having a responsible journalist on the island for a week or so would be helpful. And I felt confident that our program here could stand on its own merits."

Hendrick asked, "What makes you think you can trust me to write favorable articles?"

Farrow smiled. "Well, I figured your credentials might get in the way of your distorting our efforts here. At least, I felt certain a journalist who ranked second in a class of three hundred and twenty and is the youngest full-time staff reporter on the *Courier* would have little motivation for selling us short down here. And you'd have no motivation for telling a story that we could not live up to."

Surprised and somewhat flattered by Farrow's research on him, Hendrick also felt a subtle forewarning, as if Farrow's remarks were the exploratory jabs of a prize fighter early in the bout. It was too soon, Hendrick thought, to raise questions that he knew must be asked—penetrating questions prompted by what Hendrick had learned so far. Hendrick knew that there would be other conversations with Farrow and that he had better prepare himself for them.

"Well, I appreciate that, Dr. Farrow, and I would like to do a good job on this assignment for you."

"Good. Is the staff cooperating with you satisfactorily?"

"Yes sir—for the most part, they've been very helpful. I had a nice visit with Glen Borden and Walt Matthews the other night, and both were trying their best to make me feel less a foreigner."

"They're good men. I guess I should've sent you to Matthews right away. He's our self-appointed tour director. I used to feel a little annoyed by his enthusiasm and schemes to entertain guests of the Institute until I realized that visitors enjoyed tours with him more than with me. Consequently, except for VIP's, the tours are now his domain, and he does the job well." Farrow chuckled, "I think if I'd let him, he could have had some of those people buying land that a month later would be underwater."

"Just how big a job is it to manage the Institute?"

"It's almost getting too big for one man. I used to be able to keep up with all of our projects—know where researchers were in them daily. That included managing all the supplies, payroll, and correspondence. But we've expanded the scope of our studies to the point where I'm almost always a week behind. We actually need about two more administrative personnel—one just to handle the requisition and purchasing of equipment and supplies alone."

"You do all of that now?"

"Yes."

"What about the other personnel? Who determines who comes here?"

"You mean the students?"

"Everybody."

"Well, I select the teaching residents and permanent staff, but our students are selected by either personal recommendations from the staff or simply by application. We've had pretty good luck with those we accepted. For the most part, they are all dedicated researchers, but they're still kids, and they keep us old-timers hopping to stay up with them."

Hendrick watched Farrow intently as the latter filled a pipe with tobacco, tamped, and lit it.

"How were you able to get Dr. Stassen here?"

Farrow failed to completely disguise the concerned expression on his face. Hendrick had been waiting for it, and though Farrow quickly smiled and began to talk about Stassen, Hendrick knew that he had scored.

"That's a major coup that some of my fellow directors still can't believe I pulled off. I'd never admit it to them, but I really didn't have that much to do with it."

"How so?"

"We developed the position for a resident scientist specializing in marine toxins after Stassen came. Our salaries were so low—and still are—that to get someone like Stassen was wishful thinking. So, we simply didn't try. Then, out of the blue, Dr. Stassen wrote and said he was interested in a position here. He was getting close to retirement and, though it's conjecture, I think that he was simply trying to slow down. I guess he thought he could best do that at a place like Jaheewah. I thought we'd lose him on the salary issue, but we flew him over here, he liked the place, and I was able to hire him on the spot. When we an-

153

nounced his appointment, our status in marine biology took a quantum leap forward. We began to get requests from other institutes and some of the journals to be kept advised of developments here. Before he came, I couldn't even get our name mentioned in some of the same period-icals."

"Was there ever any jealously of Stassen—because of his prominence?"

"No. None. Everyone here recognized that he was first and foremost a scientist in the truest sense of the word. I did assign him to a private cottage, but this was the only request he ever made of me. I appreciated that. Otherwise, everything he did was 'by the book,' as it were. I gave him the same set of guidelines and procedures I give all members of the Institute, and to my knowledge, he always honored them."

"Then you and he got along all right—personally?"

Farrow obliquely glanced at Hendrick and hesitated before answering. Hendrick thought to himself, *That's right, Dr. Farrow. You're wondering how much I know, aren't you?*

"Yes. We got along fine—everything considered. He was a very private person and neither required nor desired much company in the social sense. We all understood that and let him alone."

"Margaret Courtney told me that he had no family. That none was present at the memorial service."

"That's true. I understand they were killed in the war, though items of that personal a nature were not a part of our normal interview process. I would have been grateful to have him voluntarily confide that kind of information in me but would never have asked him about it myself."

"As Head of the Institute, were you satisfied with his work here?"

"Very much so. You know, there's a kind of funny thing about personalities like Stassen's. Others' too, I guess. They add a little excitement, a little charisma, to what they're doing, and our kids—the younger students—are awfully impressionable. It's all right with me that, because of Stassen's influence, they became a little over-zealous about some aspects of their work. For example, I know that if I told you that when you tilt this pitcher of coffee far enough, coffee will pour out of it, you'd be—how shall I

155

say—'underwhelmed' to say the least. But Stassen . . . he could say the exact same thing with his German accent, and some budding young scientist in the back row of the lecture hall would mutter, 'God, he's a wizard.' And I'm very glad he served on our staff. I wish that . . . I wish things were different." Farrow paused and for a moment seemed lost in his own thoughts. Then looking towards Hendrick, he spoke again. "More coffee, Bob?"

"Yes, thanks—just a little." Hendrick decided to leave the subject of Stassen for the moment. "What is this, your ninth, tenth year as Head of the Institute?"

"Tenth year. Before that, I taught at the University. I don't remember exactly how I did it, but somehow I convinced the head of our department that since the state had just acquired the island, we ought to request a portion of it for a marine biology research station. He, in turn, convinced the Board of Regents and the Legislature. So, we were in business. It surprised the hell out of me, but they gave us the entire island. We began simply as a summer school extension study area for honor students and gradually were able to expand into our present year-round facilities with full-year graduate programs and resident staff."

"And the Randolph property became the facilities?"

"Right. We did a lot of converting of barns and cottages and stables. Those first summers were pretty rough. Days were spent studying and setting up test stations, and nights were spent knocking out walls and improving the buildings."

"Where did the money come from?"

"Grants, mostly. Occasionally, we would connect with someone who loved the island and liked our mission and so would endow a chair in his or her name, and that would help out considerably. As you might guess, labor was cheap. There were token lease payments to the state on the property, and to give you an idea of salary, the highest level on the schedule was called 'Mildly Insulting.' Most of the grant money went for supplies and food. Looking at our budget now, I can't see how we made it—but we did. And truthfully, I kind of miss those early days."

"Do you see any difference in the students of ten years ago and those on the island now?"

"Do you want the truth?"

"Sure."

"Well, you print this and I'll deny it and call you a liar. But I do. By and large, there's not the same quality of student that I remember from the earlier days. Oh, there are exceptions to that of course—Margaret's a good example—but I do see a difference. And our students here are supposedly the cream of the crop. I don't know. Memories are often clouded when we try to recall how we evaluate those early years of the Institute. That's why you'd better not print those remarks."

"I know what you mean. I read a piece of copy the other day for a fellow reporter, and it was lousy—grammar, syntax, and all. When I said something about it, he said, 'Oh well, the editors will take care of that.' He thought that it was enough just to get the story."

"You're not going to tell me that he's now the editor, are you?" They laughed and Farrow seemed to relax a little.

"No. But he's probably still putting out bad writing. Speaking of writing, I had better get back, if I'm to finish some of this stuff tonight. Seriously, I am very sympathetic to your work here and will try to do a good job—one that will please you."

"Thanks, Bob. I have every confidence that you can do a lot of good here, and I'm looking forward to reading your articles. If I can help in any way, please let me know." Farrow laid his pipe in the large ashtray and stood.

Hendrick replied, "Certainly—and thanks for the coffee and the visit."

"You're welcome, and I appreciate your coming and listening to all my propaganda."

Hendrick grinned and extended his hand. "My pleasure, and I'm sure we'll talk again. Goodnight, Dr. Farrow."

"Goodnight. Be careful in the dark. Occasionally, there's a fallen limb or two you can trip over."

"Thanks. I'll be careful. Goodnight."

Hendrick walked carefully along the pavement which led around the corner of the cottage and toward the barracks. His eyes slowly adjusted to the darkness, and he enjoyed the walk to his room. A bright moon bathed the courtyard in light, filtered through the graceful moss-draped limbs of massive live oaks. Looking toward the trees surrounding the complex, he saw one of the riding horses standing in a fenced pasture and thousands of fire-flies which emerged from the ground.

Hendrick opened the door to his room. He hesitated before the desk, deciding he would wait until morning to do any writing. It was nearly one o'clock, and the events of the day had tired him. In bed, his thoughts revolved around conversations with Margaret and Dr. Farrow. He still couldn't quite figure Farrow out. Basically, he liked the man, but at this point, he simply did not trust him. He tried to be objective about Margaret's perceptions, but they were too equivocal. There were too many questions for tonight. Tomorrow he could think more clearly. He quickly fell asleep.

CHAPTER 8

Hendrick took the phone receiver from Jackie Holcomb, Farrow's secretary, and waited until she turned away before speaking.

"Hello?"

"Bob?"

"Yes."

"It's Margaret."

"I thought so. Are you still on the mainland?"

"No. I'm calling from the lab. As a matter of fact, I can see you there at the window." Hendrick looked out the window toward the lab building. Flashing a big smile and lowering his voice, he replied, "We've got to stop meeting like this. Put your binoculars down, and I'll meet you for breakfast."

"No thanks. I've eaten already. But can you come over here now? I don't think anyone's going to be in for a while, and I've got something to show you."

"Ohhh, no! I'm not falling for the old 'come into my laboratory' routine."

"Oh, Bob. Shut up and listen. I've found something."

"Oh yeah? What?"

"I don't know exactly. Just a note—but I don't want to discuss it on the phone. Maybe you had better look at it yourself."

"Okay. I'll be right over. Can you make coffee over there?"

"Sure, if you're willing to drink it."

"I'll take my chances. Be right there." He hung up the phone and thanked Jackie.

Hendrick hurriedly crossed the courtyard in anticipation of Margaret's 'find.' Through the screen door, he saw her at one of the lab stations heating a beaker of water. He entered just as she dropped instant coffee into the beaker and began to stir the liquid with a glass rod. She wore blue jeans and a sweatshirt covered by an unbuttoned white lab jacket.

"I can't get over how different you look here than yesterday in the restaurant." Hendrick said, as he opened the door.

"Oh really?"

"Yeah. You looked very nice yesterday." He added, "Just kidding."

Reaching for a small bottle and pretending to pour from it into the beaker, she replied, "How much hydrochloric do you like in your coffee?"

Hendrick chuckled, "Have a nice evening?"

"So-so. It's a change of routine I need every now and then. We usually have dinner and take in a movie. Seriously, how do you want your coffee?"

"Black and strong."

"Good. It is that. I think I put in twice as much as I should have."

"I wonder if Madame Curie got her start this way."

"I hope you know that this stuff is bad for you anyhow."

"Yep, I do. So . . . what did you find?"

Margaret quickly reached into the large pocket of her jacket and brought out a folded piece of memo pad paper.

"This morning, I went through Dr. Stassen's office, and there was nothing there. It had all been cleaned out—desk drawers, the files—everything. The desk hadn't been moved, so I thought maybe something might have fallen down behind it. Stassen's papers and memos to himself were usually piled on top of the desk." She handed him the note. "I don't know what it means; maybe you can figure it out."

Hendrick unfolded the note and asked, "Is it possible Stassen wrote this?"

"I don't know, but I think so. It looks like his handwriting, and the 'seven' with the line through it is European. Of course, a lot of people make their sevens that way. A package I sent to Frankfort once came back undeliverable simply because they took my 'seven' to be a 'one', and there wasn't such a house number. But what do you think the note means?"

Hendrick read the note aloud: "*Shrimp Bucket. 305-460-5525. 9:00 p.m. $80,000.*" He continued, "I don't know what the 'Shrimp Bucket' is but I certainly understand 'eighty thousand dollars.' I'm sure the 305 number is a telephone."

"That's got to be right. Three-zero-five is the area code for the Miami area—it's the same as my parents'. But the rest of the number could be any place"

"Maybe 'Shrimp Bucket' is a code name for some organization."

Margaret responded, "I dunno. Could be, I guess. It could also be a restaurant, for that matter."

"Maybe Stassen was supposed to meet somebody there. Do you know if he had business interests off the island?"

"I don't know—but I doubt it."

"He was getting close to retirement. Maybe it's an investment of some kind. Did he ever talk to you about what he would do when he left here?"

"All I know for sure is that he planned to return to Europe."

"Maybe Stassen changed his mind—maybe he had decided to invest in a business or some property?" Hendrick kept voicing ideas to Margaret, hoping for something plausible.

"I just don't know." She poured coffee into two mugs and handed Hendrick one of them. They hesitated before saying anything else.

Suddenly, Hendrick remembered, "Wait a minute! Somebody told me . . . it was Glen Borden. He said that he had seen Stassen leaving the dock one night, apparently to meet some people on a big yacht." Hendrick scanned the lab and reached for the telephone, near the doorway. On a small desk were a note pad and pencils. "Can I get an outside line? I want to call the Coast Guard."

"Yes. Dial nine. Their number is posted there on the wall."

Hendrick dialed the number and sipped his coffee while waiting for an answer. He quickly shot her an expression of mock disbelief at the strength of the mixture. She responded by lightly kicking his shin. The voice came through the receiver loud enough for both of them to hear, and Hendrick held it away from his ear.

"U.S. Coast Guard. Ensign Parker speaking."

"Good morning, sir. This is Robert Hendrick of the Charleston *Courier*. I'm trying to trace the owner of a particular vessel. All I have is the name of the boat and possibly the port."

"What are they? Maybe I can still help you."

"It's the 'Shrimp Bucket', and I think she's out of Miami."

"I don't even have to look that up. I've seen her around here within the past month." Hendrick smiled at Margaret and whispered, '*Bingo!*' Parker continued, "I think she belongs to a shrimp processing and packaging company in Miami, but I'm not sure. I suggest you call the US Coast Guard Operations Sector in Miami. They will have her documented and can tell you for sure."

"Do you think she might be up for sale? I've got a price of eighty thousand dollars written here."

"Man, that's a sixty-five foot luxury yacht! You couldn't buy that boat for *six hundred* and eighty thousand."

"I guess not. Well, thanks for the information."

"Yes sir. Glad to help. And let me know if they do want to sell her for eighty grand."

"Thanks a lot. Goodbye." Hendrick hung up turned to Margaret. "Well . . . I don't guess he was trying to buy a yacht, but he obviously wanted something an awful lot to be willing to spend eighty thousand dollars for it."

"I guess so."

Hendrick reread the note carefully, rhythmically thumping the edge of the paper with his finger. "I've got another idea, if you're willing to try something."

"Sure. Whatever."

"Can you make a long distance call without going through Farrow's office—without his knowing?"

"Sure."

"Okay. Here's what you do. Call this number in Miami, and tell them you're Stassen's lab assistant, and make up something about unfinished business. Mention the eighty thousand dollars. Tell them you came across the note in his papers and wondered if it could be important. You feel okay trying that?"

"It's a little daunting, but I'll try.

"Right. Now dial the number, and hold the receiver so I can hear."

She sat at the small desk, took the note from Hendrick, and dialed for an outside line. She then dialed and waited. The phone rang once, and then a pleasant voice answered.

"Good morning. Allied Industries. May I help you?"

"Yes. I am calling in reference to a matter that someone there had with Dr. Heinrich Stassen of Jaheewah Island Marine Biology Research Institute."

"Can you be more specific? This is an international company, dear, and I don't know who would have talked with your Dr. Stassen."

"I'm not sure. You see, Dr. Stassen recently died, and I am responsible for settling his personal affairs here at the Institute."

Hendrick nodded approvingly.

"Well, let me see if I can locate someone for you through the general intercom." Margaret listened carefully and heard the secretary's voice in the background call for anyone having business with a Dr. Stassen on Jaheewah Island.

In just a moment, she spoke again.

"Miss?"

"Yes?"

"Mr. Brody of our R & E staff will talk with you if you will hold on for a while—he's on another line."

"R & E?"

"Research and Exploration department. Allied processes seafood."

"I see. Thank you—I'll hold." She quickly jotted down Brody's name and Allied Industries-R & E. In a few seconds the voice returned.

"Miss? Are you still there?"

"Yes, I am."

"Go ahead, Mr. Brody."

"With whom am I speaking, please?" His voice sounded cold and business-like.

"Abigail Johnston at Jaheewah Island Marine Biology Research Institute. I am Dr. Stassen's lab assistant."

After several seconds, Brody replied, "It was my understanding he had died."

"Yes. That's correct. But his business affairs were turned over to me to clear up, which is why I called your company."

"That was my next question. How did you know to call us?"

"Well you see, in going through his papers, I discovered a note containing your number and the figure of eighty thousand dollars." Another pause—uncomfortably longer.

"Quite frankly, Miss Johnston, I would rather not discuss my dealings with Dr. Stassen over the phone with someone I don't personally know."

"I certainly understand, but I assure you, I am responsible for all of Dr. Stassen's affairs now, and if he had business matters or obligations, I am in a position to possibly reconcile them." There was another long pause. Hendrick nodded approvingly and signaled her an "okay" gesture.

"Let me ask you, Miss Johnston, do you have access to Dr. Stassen's personal effects—specifically, his laboratory notes?"

Both Hendrick and Margaret looked surprised. Hendrick nodded approvingly, and she answered, "Yes, but may I ask why?"

"Well, Dr. Stassen and I were negotiating an agreement which I thought would now be impossible because of his death. However, if you have access to his notes, we might talk further—privately."

Hendrick pointed to the amount of money.

"And the eighty thousand?" Margaret asked.

"I'm afraid that would have to be renegotiated."

"I understand. But your company is still interested in his notes should we decide to make them available?"

"Let me say this frankly, Miss Johnston. I would like to proceed in this matter in spite of Dr. Stassen's unfortunate death. If there is some way that you can privately provide us with the notes and assure our company exclusive rights to them, I am certain that we can agree on a satisfactory figure. Do I make myself clear?"

"You would like to buy the notes and keep everything confidential?"

"Exactly," Brody replied. Hendrick scribbled on the pad 'stall.'

"I'll have to think it over."

"You do that Miss Johnston, but I would like to have an agreement soon. And I want to impress upon you the importance of your not relating this conversation to anyone. Can I expect your call say . . . within a week?"

Hendrick nodded.

Margaret answered, "Yes, I'll try to call by then. Good-bye."

Brody hung up immediately, and Margaret stared at the receiver—surprised and a little frightened by what she had heard. She nervously placed the receiver on its cradle and looked at Hendrick. "

He scared me, Bob. He really sounded ruthless."

"I know. But you did well. You did *very* well. '*Abigail Johnston*'?"

Margaret smiled, "I thought that was pretty clever."

"We've got to find those notes and quick. There must be something in there worth eighty grand, and we had better find it before someone else does."

Margaret responded, "I haven't been able to find out where his personal belongings are. I certainly can't ask Farrow. I thought Jason might know, since he probably helped clean up Dr. Stassen's cottage. But I haven't seen him to ask. As far as his files and reports, the things he kept here in the lab, they were gone the morning after they found Stassen. I'm relatively sure that Dr. Farrow had them boxed and stored in his office. I don't know if he would allow anyone to look at them or not."

"But you said you thought he personally took Stassen's notebook."

"That's right."

"So . . . maybe Farrow knew about the eighty thousand dollars Stassen was offered for it and either wants it for himself or, if that's too unethical, wants to prevent anyone else from getting their hands on the notes. In some research situations, the work done there is paid for by the organization and is considered the intellectual property of that organization."

Margaret thought for a moment then added, "I don't think Farrow's after the money. And, if he did want to sell the notebook, how would Dr. Farrow know about Mr. Sleaze at Allied Industries? I don't think he could have."

"Right. What I'd really like to know is why the notes have such a high price tag on them. Can you remember anything you've seen or heard that might tell us what is in them?"

"Not really. You see, I got in his office only occasionally to clean up for him. He was always there and simply would not discuss his work with me."

"You don't have any idea what he was working on?"

"Well, of course I knew that his field included toxic presence in invertebrates and small fishes but, specifically, I couldn't tell you what aspect he studied. He did seem to be concentrating on the shrimp, because he kept five working twenty-gallon tanks with shrimp in each. Not having his notes, I could only guess what he was doing."

"Make a guess."

"He must have been trying to set up some sort of miniature ecosystem or good food pyramid study because each of the tanks contained shrimp and also different kinds of plankton—mainly phytoplankton.

"Why do you need five different tanks with the same stuff in them?"

"Well, I don't know. I'd have to see his notes. But there seemed to be some kind of progression—like in stages. I think I mentioned this to you before."

"So the shrimp in the final tank of the series looked better?"

"Yes. They just looked fatter and I guess about as healthy as any shrimp I've seen . . . or eaten."

"Are larger shrimp more desirable—from a consumer's point of view?"

"Not necessarily. The small shrimp are awfully good. But a lot of people will buy only the large fantail shrimp."

"Let's just say for sake of argument that Stassen developed some way of producing larger shrimp and wanted to sell the idea to a shrimp processing company. Would he have to go through the Institute—through Farrow—or could he make the sale on his own?"

"I would think that if he sold the information, information that he had gathered while working here, for personal gain, Farrow would be very upset to say the least. In Stassen's case, Farrow might criticize and chastise him for ethical reasons, but that's about all that would happen."

"I guess so. But there's got to be a tie-in for Allied Industries, and I don't guess we'll know for sure until we see the notes."

"I think you're right."

"Tell me something else."

"Okay."

"Did Stassen ever talk to you about his past—about his family?"

"We had so little of that kind of conversation, it's hardly worth mentioning. In the beginning, I was really trying hard to get him out of his shell—to make him talk about anything other than his work. I guess I was really a pest." She laughed to herself. "I remember one time his saying, *'Tell me, Miss Courtney, do all American women chatter as much as you do'?*

"I just glared at him, and then he smiled—it was the first time I had ever seen him smile. Then I realized what I must have sounded like and started laughing. We laughed together, and I think it pleased him. A few days after that, he asked me what I hoped to do after leaving here. I told him that I wanted to go to Europe. This kind of casual conversation was so unlike him that I thought I had really scored. Then, I did kind of a dumb thing, I guess. I was trying so hard to make him like me. I knew from reading his CV that he grew up in Dresden—in east Germany. So, I told him that I had heard that Dresden is a beautiful city and asked if he could he tell me about it. I really hit a nerve. He said that it was the most beautiful city in Europe until our stupid Allied Forces completely destroyed it in four separate bombing raids. Thousands of innocent people were killed. And then he told me that he would not discuss personal or family matters with fellow workers—'underlings,' I think he said. That was the last conversation we had."

"And he never mentioned his family—a wife?"

"Nope. Not to me."

"Have you ever figured out just why he came to America?"

"No."

"I understood that Farrow hired Stassen after he requested a position."

Margaret was surprised. "I didn't know that."

"Farrow told me no position existed—that Stassen just came here out of the blue."

"If that's true, I would say that Farrow was certainly living right. Some of my school friends say that, at the university, this is referred to as 'the Jaheewah miracle.' I thought they meant that Farrow was just lucky in going after Stassen and getting him. But if Farrow didn't initiate the inquiry, it really was a miracle, because Stassen really put this island on the map." Margaret started to say something else but noticed Dr. Farrow at the doorway. Hendrick caught her expression of apprehension then grabbed the notepad and pencil and spoke louder than necessary.

"So, Margaret, you do enjoy the work here. What do you plan to do when you leave the island?"

Before she could answer, Farrow entered the lab and greeted them.

"Good morning, Margaret, Bob. Jackie told me you might be here."

"Come on now, Dr. Farrow. Can't a guy try to make some time with a good-looking scientist without some secretary keeping tabs on him?"

Farrow looked at Margaret then back at Hendrick. Smiling slightly, he teased, "Well, the world is full of eyes and ears, Mr. Hendrick, so we all have to mind our manners. How are things, Margaret? You finding enough to do?"

"Yes sir. I've got my own tests running, but if you need me for anything else, just let me know."

"Thank you, Margaret. I appreciate that, and I will let you know. Bob, I'm about to make a run down to the southern end of the island to see if there are any signs of turtle hatchlings getting ready to make their move to the ocean tonight. It's quite a sight when they emerge from the egg pits. I want you to see the area and meet Dr. Hatcher, our resident expert on turtles. He can tell you more than you want to know about turtles."

"Sure. Maybe we can talk again later, Margaret."

"Certainly," Margaret answered. She began to clean up the mugs and the beaker of coffee.

"You're welcome to come along, Margaret, if you'd like."

"Thanks, but I've got some tests I'm monitoring, so I'd better stay with them."

"Alright. Well, we'd better get down there, Bob."

The two men left the lab, and as they got outside, Jason and two other workers arrived in one of the vans. On the way to the beach, Farrow explained to Hendrick how the sea turtles had already laid the eggs, abandoned the area, and disguised the digging for their egg pits.

"Well, Bob, when the turtles come in to lay their eggs, they're like leatherbacks moving across the surface of the sand. You won't see this today, but when they come in to lay their eggs, it looks like an invasion of World War I helmets storming the island. After 45 to 70 days, hatchlings pip or break out of their shells but remain in their nests for a few days. They absorb their yolks which gives them the much needed energy to make their run to the water." Farrow went on to explain that at night, there are fewer dangers like birds, ghost crabs, raccoons, fish, even driftwood and deep tire ruts.

"How do the hatchlings know which way to go?" Hendrick asked.

"We assume that too is instinct. Perhaps it's the slope of the beach, the whitecaps of the waves—maybe something as simple as stars, the moon, and the natural light of the horizon." Farrow continued, "Those that safely reach the water disappear from this area. When they mature to

182

the size of a small pizza, they mysteriously return to the same area where they hatched years before. It's amazing."

Jason stopped the jeep at the opening to the beach.

"Okay, we're here," Farrow announced.

Hendrick scanned the beach where a few of the students were smoothing out the sand and dragging big pieces of driftwood from the shore, clearing the pathway to the ocean. The rest were watching waterfowl beginning to gather for an expected feeding frenzy.

Farrow spoke again and gestured toward a lanky, bearded young man who was giving instructions to the other students in preparation for the hatchlings' nocturnal appearance from their egg pits.

"Bob, let me introduce you to Dr. Hatcher. Jim, this is Bob Hendrick with the *Courier*. He's here to do some articles on the Institute. Jim is our resident authority on aquatic life in general and is a specialist on sea turtles. Jim, can you give Bob here some background on what's about to happen?"

"Sure, Dr. Farrow. Hey, Bob. Welcome to Jaheewah."

"Thanks, Dr. Hatcher." Hendrick makes a sweeping gesture. "All of this looks pretty exciting."

"Well, it is one of nature's greatest enigmas. After the turtles lay their eggs, they return to the water. Usually, the females return for the next nesting season—they take no other interest in the eggs they produced. Then, when, and if, the hatchlings make it safely to the water, they have to contend with the fish and the terns. A swimming frenzy begins. Those that make it to deep water are gone for over a decade. We consider these the *'lost years'* because no one knows where they go. We have no way to track them and no explanation for what guides them back or what dictates the time frame."

On the return trip to the Institute, the conversation was sparse. Hendrick was lost in thought about the events of the morning and was excited to have the chance later to witness this phenomenon. He could not help but see parallels between the hatchlings' fate and, however it happened, Stassen's death. Both were vulnerable. Hendrick could not deny the ambivalence he felt about Farrow. His enthusiasm for his work was obvious and clearly rubbed off on his colleagues and students. Yet Hendrick felt certain that Farrow knew what had happened to Stassen, even if he were not responsible himself. Hendrick wondered how

184

Farrow could dismiss the murder of an eminent scientist such as Stassen as easily as he might abort an inconclusive experiment.

JAHEEWAH

CHAPTER
9

Hendrick, Farrow, and Jason were back at the south beach at dusk, and it was clear there would be emerging hatchlings. The normally quiet beach would soon erupt into a battlefield—a gauntlet—staged for the turtle hatchlings' race for the sea, and life. It was as if the waterfowl and ghost crabs had received invitations for dinner—the large birds soaring high overhead and the gulls and crabs nervously pacing the shore and waiting. They patiently awaited the movement in the sand they knew would soon come. Then, it happened. The first of the hatchlings popped their heads out of the sand and began their frantic crawl to the ocean. For the next hour, the activity intensified. Students were running through the predators and hatchlings, frantically waving their towels and shirts to scare off the predators who were trying to grab the turtles before they got to the water. Hendrick watched as some of the gulls, terns, and ospreys were able to capture their victim and fly away. If there was no protection, the newly hatched, soft-shelled turtles would be easy prey. For those that made it to the water, there still were the sea predators to elude.

It had gone rather well, and only a few, too distracted from their course, too weak to run the gauntlet, met their fate. Hendrick decided that, if he left the island suspicious of some of its residents, he would also leave more aware of the critical, delicate balance of life for all its inhabitants.

The crew had all gathered for supper back at the dining hall, and much of the talk centered around the night's excitement. For these people, it seemed enough satisfaction just being participants and observing. However, the reporter in Hendrick recognized the value of the event as an attention-getting public education piece and was glad that he had stopped that morning to get his camera to get photos of the scene.

The next day, one of the men who joined them at the table for lunch was Dr. Palliston, M.D. for the Institute. He had been unable to talk to Hendrick earlier but volunteered that his afternoon was free. Together, they walked from the dining hall to the infirmary. Palliston was over six feet tall and balding but otherwise, Hendrick judged, in excellent shape for a man of fifty-seven.

Hendrick judged Palliston to be intensely dedicated to his work. Yet, conversation with him was comfortable and intriguing. Hendrick found himself answering almost as many questions as he asked. Early on in the conversation, both men discovered philosophical agreement on a wide variety of topics.

"You'll have to forgive me, Bob. I seem to have led you away from the things you're here to ask me."

"Not at all. I'm trying to get more human interest in the articles, so it's helpful just to meet the staff and draw my own conclusions."

"I see. Well . . . what would you like to know?"

"I'm interested in why a man such as yourself, who could be living in an eight or nine hundred thousand dollar home, playing golf on the weekends, and pulling down a six figure salary, would be content to spend his time on this island."

Palliston smiled and replied, "You know what I did this morning, Bob?" Hendrick shook his head. "I got up about

189

seven, took my shower, and had breakfast with my wife. We sat there and over our coffee, talked for about an hour. She had some sewing to do, so I came on over here about eight-thirty. I treated two patients for stomach problems, gave one injection, and read three articles. One of them was on new drugs and the others were about how we're developing antibiotic resistant bacteria. Damn spooky articles."

"What's that all about?"

"You'll be hearing more about it. But apparently by over-prescribing or indiscriminately using antibiotics, we are slowly developing bacteria with absolute resistance to these drugs. And we're running out of drugs to fight these super-bugs. The next stage is epidemics with nothing to effectively combat them."

"Sounds pretty frightening."

"You bet. And as a prescriber, I sure as hell need to think about it. Before I came down here from Columbia, I felt that aspect of the job, the CME, that's Continuing Medical Education, getting farther and farther away from me, and I had no time to catch up. And, of course, the paperwork was getting to me as well. You should know by now that I'm a talker, and patients like to talk and not feel rushed with their physicians. Well, there just wasn't time—there wasn't time for a conversation like this."

Hendrick was distracted by someone at the screen door. He turned and saw a black child waiting to be noticed with a soiled and torn teddy bear clutched in her thin black arms. Hendrick thought she might be seven or eight years old.

Palliston rose and greeted the little girl warmly. "Hello there, Miss Sammy. Come right in and let me see what you've got there." He opened the door for her, and she entered, almost in tears. Samantha Moser looked up at Hendrick then quickly turned away from him. She held the teddy bear for Palliston to see. The fabric across the bear's stomach was torn, and a lot of the stuffing had fallen out. Palliston took the stuffed toy and carefully laid it on the examining table. Both men were amused as the child, dressed in a t-shirt and shorts, explained the situation in a soft, slow drawl.

"My mama say we gonna have to throw him away, because he done spilt all his guts. I told her doc Jim fix my teddy up."

Palliston spoke softly. "Well, I don't know, Samantha. It looks kind of serious." He picked the little girl up and sat her on the examining table. "Maybe you had better sit up here with your teddy bear while I see what I can do. Now, where did I put my supply of teddy bear guts?" He opened the cabinet across from the table and took down a box of cotton balls. "Ah, here they are." He placed the box on the table and tucked two handfuls of the sterilized cotton into the toy. "Now we had better sew him up so he won't spill his guts again." Taking some surgical thread and a needle, he deftly sewed the tear shut and tied it off. In a serious tone, he said, "Before I let you take him home with you, I'd better check both of you over real good." Gently turning her, he smiled and continued, "You just lie down here next to your teddy bear."

Palliston pushed on the animal to rearrange the stuffing inside. He then felt the child's pulse, felt her head, and carefully ran his hands over her chest and abdomen. As he gently palpated her abdomen, she winced slightly in pain. Palliston's facial expression revealed nothing, but Hendrick sensed that something was not quite right.

"How have you been feeling, honey?"

"I been alright," the small voice answered.

"Are you sure? No tummy ache?"

"I had a tummy ache last night, but my mama make it well."

"That's good. Well, you can go on out and play now, and let me know how your teddy bear gets along. And you bring him back to see me tomorrow. Will you do that?" He gently lifted the girl off the table and handed her the teddy bear. "And both of you stay out of the hot sun most of the day. Okay?"

"Yessir, I will. Thank you, Doc Jim."

"You're welcome, honey. And have yourself a piece of candy—you know where it is." On her way out of the office, Samantha took a piece of peppermint from the tin on Palliston's desk.

Hendrick finally spoke. "You've got it pretty soft, Jim. I've never heard of malpractice suits from teddy bears."

Palliston did not smile. "No—but the child may have something. I hope to God I'm wrong."

"Something serious, obviously."

"I don't think so because of how hard I was pushing her abdomen, but if it's more than just indigestion, I will be much more concerned. I should know in a day or two. Tomorrow, I'll see how she's doing."

"If it's not indigestion, how serious is it?"

"Enough to kill her—if it's hemolytic anemia."

"Anemia?"

"Anemia is a common blood disorder, but hemolytic anemia is another matter. If the onset of hemolysis is abrupt, it can be life threatening. The body destroys the red corpuscles at too fast a rate. I've been watching her family pretty closely. Her older sister Lawanda was brought in to me with it, and I lost her. She had splenomegaly in her thoracic area, was running a high fever, had chills, the works. Hemolytic anemic is a symptom of many different diseases, and I thought I might be dealing with a sickle cell crisis. I used the drug prednisolone, a synthetic corticosteroid, and she leveled off for a couple of hours. Then it all started again and much worse. I lost her about ten o'clock the next evening. When I first saw her, I sent tissues and a blood sample to the lab at the university. Apparently, they're having a hard time with the pathology, because I still haven't heard back from them, and it's been over a week."

"Was this the kid that died a week or so before Stassen was found?"

"Yes, why?"

"Well, I was going to ask you about her. Margaret Courtney told me about it. She said that Stassen gave her father some shrimp from the lab. I wondered about food poisoning."

"That was my first diagnosis, but the whole family—nine of them—ate the same shrimp and no one else was even nauseated. The thing that puzzled me was that she looked like a textbook case of hemolytic anemia; the symptoms and blood workup were unmistakable. And also, I've seen even more advanced cases turn around radically with the use of proper drugs. I mean, this is a common treatment in the acute stages, and she responded as if I had injected her with poison. I guess we need those every now and then to remind us that we're not so damned smart as we think we are. She was a beautiful, healthy child. I just couldn't get over it."

"Do you think it wasn't the anemia?"

195

"I don't know. I just plain don't know."

In his mind, Hendrick had already formulated his next question, but he hesitated before asking it. Palliston's concern for the little girl was admirable, but he wondered what the doctor knew of Stassen's death and was not telling. Perhaps he, in some way, was caught up in the mysterious affair.

"What can you tell me about Stassen's death?"

"He apparently drowned."

Palliston's answer seemed too quick, too automatic, and Hendrick didn't understand his use of 'apparently'.

"I know that's the official word, but what do you think happened?"

"Well, I was really surprised when I first heard about it. A man of Stassen's experience in wetland environments just doesn't let himself get in difficult situations."

"So you think something else happened, like maybe he had a heart attack and passed out?"

"No. I'd rule that out pretty quickly. Every physical I ever gave him revealed a strong heart. His only problem was respiratory."

"What kind of problem?"

"Asthma. His bronchi were easily inflamed, and he had to watch himself pretty carefully. I kept him stocked up on a metered dose inhaler. He seemed to do all right with it."

"Was he taking anything else, like insulin or something that he could o.d. on?"

"No. He wasn't even borderline diabetic. Other than the asthma, he was in pretty good shape for a 68-year-old man."

"You don't suspect foul play?"

Palliston looked at Hendrick for a long while before answering. Hendrick waited patiently. He knew he was going out on a limb by raising the question of murder with so little evidence. And he wasn't really testing Palliston as much as he was trying to draw him and his experience into the picture. Hendrick liked Palliston and felt certain that his knowledge would be important whether or not he was involved in a possible murder. Palliston carefully considered what he had to say before he broke the sudden silence between them.

"Bob, I don't know you very well, but I'm going to level with you. I'm not sure that it *was* an accident. And I guess I was negligent in not calling for an autopsy before the body was cremated. My only defense is that, at the time, it seemed so obvious that he had drowned, and I was still upset about the Moser girl's death. My confidence as a diagnostician was really shaken by that, and I couldn't get it out of my mind. I did see Stassen's body and perform a cursory examination. There was nothing visibly indicative of foul play—no cuts or bruises, no unusual swelling. According to the work schedules, everybody had been accounted for, and Stassen had been completely alone."

"But now, you don't think it was an accident?"

"Let me put it this way. I have absolutely no suspicion of any person on this island. But as a doctor, you like to know for sure about these things, and I don't know what killed the Moser girl, and I don't know what killed Stassen. And that's where I am in this thing. I can't explain in my own mind exactly what happened to him."

"Well, I'm not sure of anything except that I want to know for sure what happened. And I would also like to know that if I run into something I can't handle—something medical—I can count on you for some help on it?"

"You know what you're up against there, don't you?"

"Sure. No body."

"Exactly."

"But maybe there's a back door to this thing. Maybe we can find out without him."

"I'll help you all I can. Just let me know how."

"Can I ask you about a few people?'

"Yeah—sure."

"What about Murdock?"

"Charlie Murdock? In Hagers Point?"

"Yes. The coroner."

"He's a fine fellow. Sometimes he's a little full of gas, if you know what I mean, but he's a good man. Does a good job as coroner."

"I don't think so."

"Really? Why?"

"Well, I went to see him about Stassen's death. He showed me the report which, by the way, I think he hadn't read. And when I asked for a copy, he gave me the runaround about coming back later for it. When I did, he had gone and had taken the report with him."

"I'm very surprised at that. Doesn't sound like Charlie at all. He has no reason to hide that report. I'll call him later and ask straight up what in the hell he's trying to do. I think he'll tell me."

"Good. I'd appreciate that."

"Who else are you interested in?"

"Margaret Courtney."

"Oh really? I don't blame you. She's a fine young lady, and if I were single and your age, I'd be interested too."

"That's not what I meant."

"Oh? That's too bad," Palliston chuckled. "Margaret is sharp as a tack, and from what little contact we've had, she comes across very sure of herself and down-to-earth."

"That's what I think, too. Both she and I are convinced about Stassen's death. She doesn't believe it was an accident either."

"Does she know who's involved?"

"She does have some conjecture about that, but we have nothing concrete enough to accuse anyone.

"What can you tell me about Beebo?"

Palliston smiled warmly. "You've met Beebo, have you? He's a case, isn't he?

"Yeah."

"Old Beebo . . . I don't know how old he actually is. Maybe eighty-five or ninety. But he's been on the island all his life. Farrow's got a little game he plays with Beebo to keep him occupied."

"I heard about that and also that Beebo watches for Ja-heewah—this bird-god or whatever."

"That's right. Beebo's perfectly healthy—got the lungs and heart of a thirty-year-old—but his mind quit working for him several years back. Simple things, like picking up shells, he can handle, but machines scare him to death. And if anybody yells at him or acts like they might hurt him, he goes a little berserk. A few years back, one of the younger maintenance men thought it would be fun to see Beebo run, and when he saw him on the beach, he started chasing him with the jeep. The stupid bastard scared the hell out of him. Beebo didn't quit running until he got out in the marshes. We all searched for him, and just before dark, we found him. He was curled up like a baby in the middle of the marshes, shivering from exposure, insect bites, and the trauma of the experience."

"But at least he was alive."

"Yeah. I gave him a heavy sedative, and we put him in the hospital on the mainland for a few days. Farrow looked at some nursing homes but decided he was better off out here."

"What about the man who was chasing him?"

"Farrow fired him on the spot. Put the sonofabitch off the island that night. Whether the guy knew it or not, Farrow did him a favor. Some of the young college boys were planning on taking him out for a little walk on the beach."

"Vigilante justice?"

"Yep."

"Does Beebo ever think he's seen Jaheewah?"

"He always looks at the ocean as if he's waiting for him to come in. Occasionally, Beebo will be on the beach when a light plane flies over. He gets all excited and yells that Jaheewah has come to the island. From his point of view, if it's big and it flies, it must be Jaheewah. Airplanes particularly are just beyond his comprehension. Sometimes I think he might be right. I don't see how they get the big ones, the 747's, off the ground."

"I know what you mean. Every time I get off a plane, I'm grateful for the opportunity. Well . . . I'd better get back to my room. I've got some correspondence that needs to go out tonight."

I've enjoyed your visit, Bob. And I'll do what I can about Murdock and let you know what he says."

"Great. Thanks a lot. Also, if you happen to think of anything later in regard to Stassen, let me know. I don't imagine you have any idea what he was working on?"

"No, not really. Other than during his physicals, I recall talking at length with him only once or twice."

"What where those conversations like?"

"I do remember once we got to talking about epidemics. He said that he had worked for some time on poisonings in sea environments—things like the red tide, which nobody really understands. I loaned him some books I had on epidemic diagnosis and control, but I got them back and we never discussed it again."

"Well, he's turning out to be a real puzzle. Listen, I'd better go. Thanks for the visit."

"My pleasure."

"Oh, and by the way, since you are curious about how Stassen died, let me ask you this: do you think it's possible for someone on his back for two hours in less than four inches of water to drown?"

"I would find that hard to believe."

"So did I. But I've looked at the area Stassen was monitoring at low tide, and that's the way it was. That's why I've
got to have another cause of death before I'll be satisfied.
When you see a copy of the coroner's report, let me know
if something doesn't look quite right to you, too. Thanks
again. I'll see you later."

"All right. I'll talk with you after I hear from Murdock."

Hendrick left the clinic and walked to the barracks.
Reasonably certain of Palliston's integrity, he felt that he
could rely on him when the chips were down. Yet, Hendrick's first perceptions of the island and its inhabitants
called into question the idea of a murder here. Even now,
sure that Stassen did not drown, Hendrick felt a strong de-
sire to prove himself wrong instead of right, as if the best
thing would be for him to finish his articles and leave—to
leave the island and allow the bird-god Jaheewah to ex-
pose and rid the island of its evil.

JAHEEWAH

CHAPTER

10

Hendrick excused himself from supper and left the dining hall with no particular notice being paid him. At least, so he thought. Jason, however, sat quietly—very much aware of Hendrick's departure. Outside, Hendrick hesitated a moment before casually walking through the courtyard to the cottages on the other side of the barracks.

At the end of the walkway, like a piece of forbidden fruit, Stassen's cabin awaited, still locked and vacant. Hendrick had always left breaking and entering to more idealistic, overzealous, and ambitious reporters, but he felt irresistibly drawn to the cottage by what it might contain. He had to admit that the slight rise of adrenalin, though surprising, was enjoyable. Weighing the likelihood of being caught against finding some link to Stassen's death, Hendrick decided he must get in. Inserting a credit card eased the latch back, and the door effortlessly opened.

Moonlight dimly lit the front room of the cottage—the living room—bare except for a dusty, overstuffed couch against the front window and a desk and chair next to the opposite wall. Doorways led to a small bedroom and kitchenette. The bedroom contained only a single bed and bookshelves around three walls. Hendrick lifted the mattress and bedcovers but found nothing. The kitchenette appeared equally vacant, and Hendrick returned to the living room and sat at the desk. Opening drawers of a dresser revealed nothing—they had been emptied as well. Almost by instinct, he pulled the top drawer completely out and felt inside the opening. His fingers touched something—a piece of paper—stuck to the bottom of the slot. Even before he saw it, he could feel emulsion on one side of the paper as well as more adrenalin pouring into his system. It was a photograph—at least half a photograph—a young woman, in happy times, judging from the expression on her face. The right half of the photograph was torn away. Hendrick viewed the picture carefully, holding it towards the window to catch as much of the moonlight as possible. The complete photograph was of a couple, holding hands in front of a tree, outside a nondescript building. The larger hand, holding the small hand of the girl's, and a small portion of a white sleeve were all that remained of what was obviously a man's image. Hendrick studied at the face of the girl. She looked to be in her late twenties and about seven months pregnant.

Hendrick then turned his attention to the wall before him. It was then that he noticed a small nail. Right before him, the nail now supported nothing. Hendrick's eyes quickly saw twenty or thirty nails where pictures had been but were now gone.

A sound outside the cottage distracted Hendrick, and he quickly retreated into the bedroom and listened intently. Suddenly, a bright light shone into the front window. Hendrick looked for a some escape and then saw something that intrigued him more than fear of getting caught. The bedroom walls were covered with the same small nails he had seen in the living room. There were so many that little wall space would have been left. A man appeared in the doorway with a bright flashlight, focused on Hendrick.

"Oh, it's you, Mr. Hendricks."

"Jason, what in the hell are you trying to do, blind me?"

Jason lowered his arm and flashed instead that same grin Hendrick remembered from the dock when they first met.

"Excuse me, Mr. Hendricks. I just wanted to make sure it was you in here an' not some drunk fool with a gun. You lookin' for anythin' in particular, Mr. Hendricks?"

Hendrick remembered the photograph in his hand and nonchalantly slipped it into his windbreaker pocket.

"Just looking, Jason. Where are all of Stassen's things?"

"What do you mean, 'things'?"

"You know, clothes, books, and pictures?"

"I imagine Doc Farrow can tell you, since that's where we done took 'em."

"You mean everything?"

"Yep. He sent me over here an' said clean it out—everythin'—an' bring it all to his office."

"When was that?"

"The day after Stassen washed up on the beach."

"What did Farrow do with all the stuff?"

"Beats me. We just set it down in his office an' left."

210

"Do you remember anything unusual?"

"Like what?"

"Pictures—or some other things on the wall, maybe."

"There was a lot of stuff on the wall, but I didn't figure it was any of my business to keep account of it. Why are you so curious about his belongin's?"

"It seems to me that Farrow was in a big hurry to get control of Stassen's personal effects. That's all."

Jason hesitated before replying.

"Well, why don't you just ask him, seein' as how he wants to talk with you anyhow?"

"When?"

"Now. At least he said I was to ask you to pay him a visit whenever you get through here."

"Just curious, Jason. How did he know I was here?"

With a sly grin Jason replied, "Now, Mr. Hendricks, don't you imagine he's got ways of knowin'?"

"And you're one of them."

"An' I'm one of them. You 'bout ready, Mr. Hendricks?"

"Okay Jason—let's go see the man."

They left the cottage and walked toward the courtyard. Weaving shadows of live oak branches swaying in the moonlight formed eerie shapes on the lawn. Innocuous shadows easily resembled snakes or silhouettes of birds flying low to the ground. The Spanish moss hanging heavily in the humid night air looked almost sinister.

"Let me ask you something, Jason."

"Shoot."

"What will you do if the Institute goes under?"

"Fish."

Hendrick grinned. "No, really. If the legislature shuts this place down, won't all of you have to leave the island?"

"I imagine most of the college people will leave, but whatever they put here's gonna need lookin' after. Otherwise, it'll all grow up natural an' take over everythin'—like it was before people started messin' with it. I ain't worried 'bout that, though. Farrow's got too much going here for them to take it away from him."

212

"What do you mean?"

"I mean what I said," Jason teased. "Now if you don't understand it, I'll explain it to you. Just look around you. All them buildin's was fallin' in when Farrow got here. Now they're in first class shape, an' the grounds, is too. I don't know what that scientific stuff costs, but I sure as hell know what a fancy boat sells for—an' tractors—we got eight of them. Me an' the H.I., we got ourselves an' understandin': I don't ask for nothin' I can make do without, an' Farrow gets me whatever I ask for."

"No matter what it costs?"

"How much it costs don't really concern me if I got to have it to do the job. That's his worry."

When they reached the fountain in the courtyard, Jason stopped to light a cigarette. Hendrick watched him carefully as the flame illuminated deep lines in his leathery face. Jason doused the flame in the fountain and put the wet matchstick in his pocket.

"Mr. Hendricks, you know the way, so I'm gonna go try to talk the cooks out of some more biscuits an' coffee. Farrow said to tell you, they ain't no place on this island you can't go. So, when you get ready to break in someplace else, just remember I probably got the key. That way, I don't have to sneak up on you."

"Thanks. I'll remember that."

As Jason disappeared into the moving shadows, Hendrick made his way toward Farrow's cabin. Lights were on in the living room, and as before, the front door stood open. Hendrick started to knock when a voice from inside called.

"Is that you, Bob? Come in." Farrow came to the door wearing a khaki jacket and holding his hand-carved meerschaum pipe. He looked quite distinguished, and Hendrick stifled a terrific urge to say 'yes, bwana.'

"Thank you. I understand you wanted to talk with me."

"Yes, yes I did. Will you sit down? I'm going to have some hot tea. Will you join me?"

"No thanks. Dr. Farrow, why don't we just play it straight with one another? You've summoned me here, and I've come. So . . . what's on your mind?"

"Well now, Bob—I apologize if my request to talk with you sounded like a summons." Farrow reached forward to

214

pour himself some tea. "But I must confess, I'm wondering what's on your mind that would make you feel the need to break into one of our buildings. Now don't get me wrong— no harm's been done. I just thought we ought to have a talk about it."

"I see."

"Let me explain myself, Bob. You are a guest on this island and someone who can do for us things we can't do for ourselves. We appreciate that, and I personally want to extend to you every courtesy I can. That would include seeing anyplace on the island you want to go—anyplace. All you need do is ask. But I would appreciate your asking if for no other reason than so that you will have no difficulty or interference. All I want to do is make things more easily accessible to you."

"Forgive me, Dr. Farrow, but that sounds an awful lot like control rather than courtesy."

Farrow smiled. "I guess in a way it does appear that I'm controlling things, but believe me, Bob, I certainly have not tried to direct your activities while you are here. I must honestly tell you that I have a few people working for us who constantly try to put something over on me. If I'm not on top of everything that goes on here, then they get the notion I wouldn't notice an unusual increase in our fuel consumption or cleaning supplies, or who knows what. When I do, my hands are tied, and I have to let otherwise good help go."

"And that's why I'm here tonight?"

"No, of course not. I didn't ask you here to chide you for breaking into the cottage. I'm sorry you felt you had to. I'm just saying that I've made it clear to my staff that I want to know everything that goes on here. I can't afford surprises. And I am sorry if you felt spied upon or restricted in some way. I'll speak to Jason about it if you feel he wasn't courteous."

"Frankly, Dr. Farrow, it doesn't matter to me personally how you run this island. What does matter to me is this feeling I have that something is going on, and I can't quite put it together . . . yet."

"And that's what took you to the cottage?"

"Yes. Stassen's cottage. Now, that's twice you've referred to the cottage, but not as his cottage. Why is that?"

"I'm sorry, it's been called 'the cottage' since long before Stassen arrived, and we've gotten used to calling it that. Were you looking for anything in particular?"

"Just let me ask you—point blank. I'm very interested in Stassen. I want to know everything about him I can. Is there some reason that learning about him is a threat to the Institute or to you personally?"

"Of course not."

"Then you'll help?"

"If I can."

"You're not just stringing me along, are you?"

Farrow looked puzzled and shook his head. "Bob, I don't know what I've done or said to arouse in you such distrust, but I assure you I'll do everything I can to get this resolved to our mutual satisfaction. What do you want to know?"

"Were you ever in Stassen's cottage when he was alive?"

"Once or twice."

"Why just once or twice? I would have thought his reputation and your position would bring you together more often than that."

"I think I told you earlier that Dr. Stassen made it very clear—in fact, his acceptance of the position was contingent upon a high degree of privacy, which I, of course, granted."

"What was in the cottage?"

"You mean furnishings?"

Hendrick was beginning to tire of Farrow's apparent evasiveness. "I mean, what was in the damn cottage? You've got all of his personal belongings stored— somewhere. What's there?"

"Books and papers, mostly."

"And pictures?"

"Yes, he had a lot of photographs."

"I'll say. There must be fifty or sixty of them. Whose pictures are they? Who's in them?"

"I assume his relatives and family, but they represent his personal life, and we had agreed to avoid these areas of familiarity in our relationship."

"Do you have the photographs?"

"Some."

"May I see them?"

"Whenever you like—they're in my office."

"How about now?"

Farrow smiled. "How about tomorrow morning? It's eleven-thirty now."

"Okay. But why did you confiscate them?"

"Now there you go again, Bob. I didn't confiscate them. They're in my office for safekeeping; that's all."

"And no one from his family claimed them?"

"That's right. And we don't expect anyone to claim them. When Stassen first came and accepted the position, he brought me an envelope to be kept in our safe until he either left the Institute or something happened to him. I asked him what it contained. He said 'just papers that would be needed if certain circumstances arose.' I assumed he meant if he died. So, when he did die, I felt obliged to open the envelope. It contained a letter, which I can show you, explaining that no living relatives remained for whom personal belongings need be kept. His scientific work was to be catalogued and stored here. And finally, he left a will in which he specified that he wished to be cremated and have his ashes scattered at sea. There were also some requests related to the dispensation of royalties which you can read as well. So we gave his clothes away, put most of his books in our library, and destroyed most of the personal papers."

"You still have letters?"

"Yes, a few."

"May I see them?"

"If you like. There are a few letters that are extremely personal, and I would have to have a good reason before I could allow them to be made public."

"Dr. Farrow, are you satisfied that Stassen did drown?"

"As opposed to what?"

"I don't know. Heart attack maybe."

"I guess I'm satisfied in that Charlie Murdock, the co-roner, says that he drowned—he ought to know. If it was a heart attack, I can't see that it really matters now, since no one was around to help him."

"Well, let me tell you a few things and see how you feel about them."

"All right."

"In the first place, I've talked with your illustrious coun-ty coroner, and not only is he uncertain about how Stassen died, but also admitted to me he did not view the body himself."

"I know that. His assistant—Halston, I think is his name—did the work-up and final report. Murdock just re-lied on his judgement and okayed the report."

"But Murdock is the coroner—not some medical stu-dent. I just find it hard to believe that the body of an inter-nationally known scientist would be relegated to some second-semester med student assistant."

"I'm sure Murdock has every confidence in the young man, or he wouldn't have hired him. As a matter of fact, at the hearing, Halston presented a very thorough report on his findings. I wouldn't want to be quoted, but his report considerably bettered Murdock's usual postmortems. As far as Stassen's eminence, the average person on the mainland couldn't care less who Stassen was or, for that matter, that he worked on Jaheewah and drowned here."

"He didn't drown."

"What?"

"He didn't drown, damn it. I've seen Halston's report and, if it's accurate, as you've implied, then Stassen didn't drown."

"How do you know this and Charlie doesn't?"

"That's what I'm trying to tell you. I've covered an awful lot of police reports, and I know what certain things mean. Murdock did a shabby job on this one, and what's more, he knows it. Now, he's either scared, stupid, or he's covering up something."

"Murdock? I'm sure you're mistaken."

"Am I? I saw the report and asked him for a copy. He said to come back later, and he would have it for me. I went back, and he was gone. His secretary knew nothing about it, and when we looked for the report, *it* was gone. He obviously did not want that report seen again." Farrow reacted to Hendrick's comments with a puzzled expression. Hendrick studied his face intently. Farrow's response was one that Hendrick had noticed before—one that revealed a displeasure in learning information he felt should have come to him earlier. Hendrick wanted desperately to understand Farrow's reticence and continued to push the issue.

"If he didn't drown, maybe he did have a heart attack. But Palliston tells me his heart was in excellent shape."

"Level with me, Bob. Where are you going with this? What do you think happened?"

"I am in no position to accuse anyone, but I think he was set up somehow."

"Set up? You think Stassen was *murdered*?"

"Yeah. I sure do."

Farrow laughed incredulously. "Good Lord, Hendrick, you're sitting on an almost uninhabited island within a community of dedicated scientists and a few support staff members, and you're telling me you think Stassen was murdered? By whom?"

"I don't know yet. But it takes at least two people to bring off a murder—the killer and the victim, and one of them left to cover it up. If you think that couldn't happen on your cozy little island, then you're not very perceptive, or you're incredibly naive. And, for the record, I find you very perceptive and realistic about situations and people."

"I'll take your observation as a backhanded compliment, but I must tell you frankly that I do not share the suspicion with which you seem to be so preoccupied. And I'm going to have to see more than some confusing or inept coroner's report before I throw up a red flag and yell 'murder.' Bob, I am a damn good judge of character, and I personally hire anyone who works here. There are no murderers on this island."

Hendrick paused then continued, "Dr. Farrow, I think you honestly believe that, and there's a chance you might be right, at least about who might have murdered him. But

I don't really know any of you, and maybe I see some things more clearly, more objectively."

"Let me say this, Bob. You are a newspaperman looking for something—foul play, whatever. And if you find it, then more power to you. But if you don't find anything other than an unfortunate death, you can probably create enough suspicion and bad publicity to damage the Institute's reputation whether you intend to or not. I'm not saying back off. Not at all. I'm just saying—I'm asking you to be careful."

"That's fair enough. And I'm asking you for your help. As Head of the Institute, you owe it to Stassen to remove all doubt."

"I agree. Now, Bob, if you wouldn't mind, I'm suddenly very tired. I want to think about this conjecture of yours. I don't mind telling you I'm very concerned about what this could mean to the Institute. If you want to see Stassen's files in the morning, I'll have them ready for you about nine or so, if that's all right with you."

"That's fine. I'll be there."

Farrow stood but made no parting gesture: no pleasantry, no handshake. Obviously, Hendrick had stunned him.

Hendrick excused himself and walked away from Farrow's cottage.

Hendrick's thoughts totally absorbed him, and he felt a little confused by Farrow's demeanor and response. He seemed sincerely distraught that murder might have happened on the island. Or was he concerned that Hendrick already knew too much? How close were Farrow and Murdock? Hendrick did not remember the walk to the barracks. Even the constant sounds of the night failed to break his concentration. Well . . . now Farrow knew. And they could never talk together again the same way as before.

CHAPTER

11

"Good morning, Mr. Hendrick. Dr. Farrow said you would be in this morning."

Hendrick had had very few conversations with Jackie Holcomb but judged her to be extremely efficient, courteous, and intelligent. She had celebrated her twenty-fourth birthday the preceding week and insisted on Hendrick's presence for cake and coffee in the office. Jackie Holcomb enhanced the office with her appearance as well as her manner, conveying to an outsider the impression that Farrow's office could just as well be a corporate executive's on Wall Street.

"And how are you, Mr. Hendrick?" She wore a maxi length skirt, and her dark print blouse made her light blonde hair and deep tan even more striking.

"Fine, Jackie. Dr. Farrow said he would show me some of Stassen's personal effects this morning. Is he here?"

"No sir. He had to go to the mainland for a meeting. But he did leave some of Dr. Stassen's things for you on the desk there behind that partition." Reaching into her top desk drawer, she withdrew a manila envelope marked *Stassen—Personal.*

"He said I should show this to you only and that you should take as much time as you like with it and other things in the box. He did ask that you leave them here when you're through."

Hendrick looked at the envelope and noted a large pasteboard box on the desk behind the partition.

"Is this it? Is this all that's left?"

"Oh no, sir. These are just some personal things Dr. Farrow thought you were most interested in. There is also a four-drawer filing cabinet of scientific data which you can look through if you care to. Also, all of his books are boxed and ready to be catalogued and placed in the library."

"I'll start with these. Thank you, Jackie. May I use the desk?"

"You certainly may. And how about some fresh hot coffee?"

"That would be excellent—black, please."

"You got it. I'll be right back."

Hendrick sat at the desk and began emptying the box of its contents. Jackie returned and set a steaming mug of coffee before him.

"Here you are, Mr. Hendrick. Before I leave you alone, Dr. Palliston left a message for you to see him this morning if you could. He'll be in his office until noon. And also, you have some mail."

"Thank you. Oh . . . could you please call Palliston for me and tell him I'll stop by in about an hour?"

"I'll be glad to." She placed a letter and a picture postcard on the desk beside him. "Let me know if there is anything else I can get you."

"Thanks, I will."

She crossed to her desk and, after calling Dr. Palliston, began typing. Hendrick picked up the postcard. It had been forwarded from the newspaper as all of his first class mail had been. The *Courier* building façade pictured on the card immediately amused and puzzled Hendrick, for it had been mailed from London. He read the message from some friends—fellow reporters—who, recently married, were now on their honeymoon in the British Isles:

Hey, Bob,

None of the sights we've seen can hold a candle to that shining beacon of truth depicted on the other side. However, we will keep on looking. Saw the Tutankhamun exhibit at the British Museum yesterday. Incredible!! See you in two weeks.

Russ and Tracey

Hendrick grinned. He thought to himself, *Europe will never be the same.* The letter, written on *Courier* stationery, was from Bill Seeber, whom he had asked to research the bombing of Dresden. He scanned Seeber's handwritten note. It identified the attached four pages of typewritten copy as a short but thorough description of four Allied Forces aerial bombing attacks on Dresden over two days in

February, 1945. They dropped over 3,900 tons of high explosive bombs and incendiary devices on the city. Hendrick read the manuscript carefully, then folded the papers and put them in his jacket pocket.

Turning to the box, Hendrick withdrew the first of twenty or so framed photographs. Nearly all were black and white 8 x 10's. Most pictured a young woman in her late twenties or early thirties. A few documented the pregnancy and birth of a child. Although there remained no duplicate of the picture Hendrick had found in the cabin, the girl's identity in these confirmed the original. Two showed a man whom Hendrick recognized immediately as Stassen, younger than in the literature he had seen on the Institute, but unmistakably Stassen. These pictures revealed not an unfeeling, cold scientist but an adoring father playfully holding his child above him. *How old were these photographs?* he thought. *And where were they taken?* He noticed something written in the margin of one picture. Taking the picture out of the frame, Hendrick saw:

"Dresden, February, 1945."

Hendrick reread the letter from his friend outlining the Dresden blitz. The picture placed Stassen's family in Dresden when it suffered such devastating destruction. Though

231

the city center received the brunt of the bombs, some of the buildings did not suffer direct hits. But three of the most beautiful churches were severely damaged; including the eighteenth-century Frauenkirche, the Hofkirche, and the Kruezkirche. *What a senseless act of aggression,* Hendrick concluded.

Hendrick set the photographs aside and lifted a stack of loose papers from the box. The bulk of these consisted of certificates from various academies and universities throughout Europe, acknowledging the programs of study completion of or granted special awards. Hendrick sifted through nearly thirty letters of commendation for Stassen's achievements in the fields of marine and microbiology. A bound compilation of similar papers formed a current resumé of Stassen's work but omitted any reference to his personal life and family relationships.

Hendrick thumbed through the folder and started to replace it, then noticed two small letter-sized envelopes, both addressed to "Frau Heinrich Stassen," but with no postage or postmark. Unlike other correspondence in the box, they seemed relatively fresh. Upon opening the first letter, Hendrick saw that it was dated and apparently written only a month or so before Stassen's death. The second letter predated the first by only a few days. This must be his wife! *Why would he write to his wife knowing that she was dead?* Hendrick paused to think, carefully sipping the hot coffee. Were there other letters? Did Farrow overlook these? At the risk of upsetting Farrow, he decided to keep one of the letters and placed it in his pocket. He returned the rest of the materials to the box and got up to leave the office.

"Are you through, Mr. Hendrick? Would you like to see Dr. Stassen's files now?"

"No thanks, Jackie. I'll look through those later. Will Dr. Farrow return to the office today?"

"Dr. Farrow said if he didn't get out of his meeting in time to catch the 1:05 run, it would be after five o'clock, so he would probably go on to his cottage."

"Well, if he does come in, please tell him I was here and that there are a couple of things I'd like to ask him. Oh . . .by the way, where is Stassen's lab notebook?"

Jackie looked puzzled but not apprehensive.

"Notebook? I don't believe I've seen one, Mr. Hendrick."

233

"Hmm . . . Dr. Farrow hasn't mentioned it?"

"No sir, he hasn't."

"Well, I'll ask him about it when I see him. Thanks for the great coffee." She smiled and wished him a good day.

Hendrick opened the door to leave and noticed one of the maintenance trucks slowly rounding the drive in front of the office building. In the truck's bed, a gasoline-powered machine chugged away, spraying a fine mist that slowly settled on the shrubbery and grounds in the area.

"What is that foul-smelling stuff?" Hendricks asked Jackie.

"Isn't it terrible? It's insecticide. We really need it here on the island. If we didn't spray, the mosquitoes would eat you alive."

"That bad, huh?"

"Yes. In the summer, we have to have the area sprayed almost every other day. Everyone stays inside while it settles. Dr. Stassen even ran in here once to get away from it. Poor man, he looked scared to death. Last year, a horrible swarm of mosquitoes appeared on the mainland. They

234

traced them to one of the islands and found a drainage canal where millions of them had bred and hatched. They . . . were . . . *monsters!*"

"Really?"

"Really! Some of the men who went in there to spray were very allergic and nearly died from the bites."

"I guess the smell is worth it, then. Thanks a lot—I'll probably see you tomorrow."

"You're welcome, Mr. Hendrick. Goodbye."

Hendrick stepped out of the office and closed the door behind him. Insecticide fumes hung heavily in the moist air around the courtyard. Hendrick could still hear the truck beyond the lab building across the courtyard from where he now stood. Grateful that the infirmary lay in the opposite direction, Hendrick hurried to keep his appointment with Dr. Palliston. He knocked on the screen door and roused Palliston, who sat reading at his desk.

"Bob! Good morning. Come in, come in."

"Hi, Doc. How's it going?"

"Fine. I thought you might be interested in a couple of things I've been working on."

"Sure. What have you got?"

"You remember the little Moser girl who popped in here the day we first talked?"

"The one whose sister died?"

"Yeah. Well, this doesn't have anything to do with Stassen, but when you questioned his death, it got me thinking again about the Moser girl. Before she died, I sent some cultures to the pathology lab at the university for some help with the diagnosis. I didn't hear anything from them before we lost her. I figured it must have been something else and waited for their explanation. Well, the lab report came yesterday and it's highly unusual. My colleague there tells me that first of all, she definitely did not have a hemolytic anemia. He says the reason they took so long was that the disease was clearly viral, but they couldn't identify it. It is either some unknown virus or a strange mutant. He said if the girl survived, it would be only through inherent immunity, because the only two or three anti-virals we have did not phase it. They could be wrong about the virus, but I doubt it."

"A virus?"

"Yep. But that doesn't exactly make sense either. We're kind of a cloistered environment here and, in her case, she had little if any contact with the outside. If it had been a virus, there should be other cases. You remember her sister, Samantha? She has been sick but nothing as severe as Lawanda. And Sammy's fine now."

"And you don't see any relationship to Stassen's death?"

"No. Nothing concrete. But that's the other thing I wanted to tell you. I went to see Murdock and got a copy of the coroner's report for you. He's as embarrassed as hell and told me that he would talk with you any time you like."

"What did he say about running off with the report?"

"He just panicked, he said. He figured he had really made a mess of things and that you would blow up the story in the *Courier*. He thought this would no doubt cost him the election and maybe even hurt his business. So, he said he needed time to think and took it. He's probably telling he truth. He is kind of a panicky guy under unexpected pressure."

"Have you read the report?"

"Yep."

"Do you think he drowned?"

"Nope. At least not until he was nearly dead from some other cause. Now, if he passed out or was paralyzed in very shallow water, he might have taken in enough to drown, but the location of the lividity suggests he died on his back."

"That's what caught my eye, too. Did you see the body when he was found?"

"Yes."

"And you saw nothing unusual?"

"Nope. He washed up on the beach as clean as a whistle. I just figured he might have gotten too hot, passed out, then drowned when the tide came in."

"And you found him on the south end of the island?"

"Right. He had some estuarine test plots down there. The tide took him out to the channel between Jaheewah and the south island, then brought him back on the beach."

"What about sharks?"

"They've killed so many in that area that the sharks avoid it. And there would have been no blood or thrashing about to attract them."

"I don't know why . . . but I just don't think it's this cut and dried. In working up the story on Stassen's contribution to the Institute, I've learned that everybody viewed him as very private and often rude, but the man was obviously shrewd . . . and thorough. I don't think he would consciously put himself in jeopardy. Now, if he got into something totally unexpected—something for which he had no defense, then that's a different story."

"But, I don't know what that would be. There's nothing down there but a shallow estuary, bordered by some sand bars and the island itself."

Hendrick hesitated then asked, "And the tide water drains to the ocean?"

239

"Well, not entirely. There are a couple of little canals leading into the island and the inland waterway on the other side."

Hendrick remembered his conversation with Jackie Holcomb. "You mean drainage canals?"

"Yeah."

"Jackie told me about how bad the mosquitoes get at times and about having the area sprayed. Could Stassen have stirred them up and been bitten enough to die?"

"No. The mosquitoes are bad but not that bad. As a matter of fact, he would more likely have died from the insecticide itself."

"*What*? What do you mean?"

"I said he would be more susceptible to the fumes."

"What are you saying?"

"Didn't I tell you he was asthmatic?"

"Yes. I remember you did."

"Well, his asthmatic condition wouldn't allow him to be anywhere near the amount of insecticide they spray."

"That's right. Jackie said she had seen Stassen try to avoid it from the trucks. You mean it could actually kill him?"

"Hell, yes! One strong whiff of those fumes, and his airways could have swelled up like a balloon—completely shutting off any air passage. It would be, physiologically, like what we call 'status asthmaticus.' The bronchi become obstructed by plugs of mucus. Arterial oxygen levels fall to dangerously low levels, and carbon dioxide levels increase dramatically. The heart stops beating, and it's all over."

"But wouldn't that show up visibly?"

"Only in an autopsy. And no one requested or felt the need for an autopsy. However, I still don't think that he would've died from the spraying. That's a very open area down there, and insecticide from even a hundred yards inland would probably dissipate to a tolerable level before reaching him."

Hendrick said nothing for a while then leapt to his feet. Excitedly, he said, "That's it! By God, that's it. I'll get back with you later. I've got to check something out in a hurry."

Standing at the door, he pointed in the direction of Farrow's office. "You're sure that spray would have killed him?"

"No doubt about it. If those fumes reached him and he didn't have his inhalers with him . . ."

"*Good Lord*," Hendrick muttered, leaving Palliston's office. "*The poor bastard was a sitting duck.*"

CHAPTER
12

Hendrick walked briskly to the lab, his mind racing. He would need help, and Margaret was his best ally. Hendrick burst in, startling an unsuspecting and busy Margaret Courtney. She placed her hand on her chest and feigned a heart attack.

"Bob! You scared me!"

"Sorry, Margaret. But I'm glad to see you're alone. We don't have much time, so just listen and trust me. Okay?"

"Sure."

"Where's Beebo—right now?"

"Beebo? I don't know."

"Doesn't he look for shells on the beach during the day?"

"Yes. But he could be anywhere."

"I thought he had a regular routine. Jason—or some-body—told me you could set your watch by him."

"Gee, I don't know Bob." She paused, thinking. "Wait a minute. I've heard Dr. Farrow tell the maintenance men to be sure to get some shells out to the south beach before noon because Beebo goes down there in the afternoon. I guess that's where he would be."

"Perfect! Let's just hope he is. Now, here's what I need for you to do. Call the spraying service, and tell them that Farrow asked you to order a pilot to treat the south end of the island."

"Spraying?"

"Right. Insecticide. Tell them anything believable. Tell them . . . hell, I don't know. Give me a scientific reason to spray a beach area."

Margaret thought for a moment. "Well, I could say we're testing for the effects of ocean air currents on the spray dispersion."

"Good. You're something else, you know that? Do you think the service will question your ordering the spraying?"

"I don't think so. Sometimes Jackie just confirms it, since it's more or less regularly scheduled."

"Okay then. Now, set it up for about 1:30 this afternoon. Beebo and I will be on the south end of the island. Tell the pilot he is to look for two people on the beach down there. Tell him we are two scientists and that he's to come in low—maybe only fifty or seventy-five feet—and spray right before he's over us so we can see what the wind does. Just once is all we need. If I'm right about Beebo, I think we'll only have one shot at this, so it's got to be right."

"But Bob, this is crazy—it will scare Beebo."

"I expect it to—but I'll be there to watch him. I have to see how he reacts."

"Okay. I trust you. But you'll have to be very careful with him. Why involve Beebo anyway?"

245

"Because. I think he's the only one who saw Stassen die. He's our eyewitness. Even if he is a little crazy, he can still confirm what I think happened."

"You mean that Dr. Stassen was killed from a plane?"

"I can't explain the whole thing to you now, but I'm sure that's it. I'm still hung up on a motive, but I think he was set up just as sure as I'm standing here."

Hendrick glanced at the digital clock on the lab table. It read 11:36. "We've got to hurry. It'll probably take me at least an hour to locate Beebo without asking a lot of questions. We'll be on the south end of the beach like I said. If we're not standing on the south end of the island, it'll mean I couldn't find Beebo in time to get down there. So tell the pilot we are observing from a distance and to go ahead and release the spray. Oh . . . Farrow's off the island until at the very earliest two o'clock, so don't worry about him. Now, if it comes down to it, you're going to have to deny making the arrangements—I will tell Farrow I ordered the spraying. I've got to go now. Call the spraying service as quickly as you can manage it. And Margaret, I know you're concerned about Beebo, but I will look out for him. I promise."

"Okay. I'll do the best I can."

"Good. By the way, have you got a clipboard or a note-book I can borrow, anything to make me look scientific?"

"Sure. Take this one. Now get yourself some blue jeans with the legs cut off, and you'll look like a real marine biol-ogist."

"Very funny, Margaret. I'll see you tonight after supper and explain everything, okay?"

"Yeah. I'll be on the barracks porch."

Hendrick took the large clipboard and left Margaret in the lab. Remembering that he had not seen Beebo for a few days, he nonchalantly mentioned his absence to one of the maintenance men standing outside the dining hall.

"Beebo?" the man responded. "Oh yeah, he's around. I just seen him headin' down the road to the south end of the island."

Hendrick stepped into the dining hall, drew himself a mug of coffee and selected a sweet roll. He wanted to avoid arousing suspicions about his intention to follow Beebo and took a few minutes to eat and drink. Then, he easily

247

slipped out a door of the hall and began walking to the south beach. He looked over his shoulder fully expecting to see Jason following him in the jeep, but he continued alone on the roadway.

He found the dirt road leading through the tree-lined edge of the beach. Passing between high vine-covered dunes, Hendrick could not see Beebo. In the distance, shrimp boats gracefully bobbed on the horizon, sometimes disappearing behind a swell. Flags of sea gulls followed each boat—competing for shrimp that slipped through the nets as they cleared the water's surface.

Hendrick turned to walk back to the path. In the recess between two dune hills sat Beebo, curiously eyeing Hendrick. He had walked within ten feet of Beebo and had not noticed him. Beebo, sitting quietly, looked first at Hendrick then at shells he carefully removed from his brown paper sack. Hendrick smiled broadly and slowly approached the old black man.

"Hello, Beebo. You finding a lot of shells today?" Beebo said nothing but watched Hendrick's approach intently.

"You remember me, Beebo? I'm Bob. Remember?"

"I know you. You man want to talk. See the shells? Nice shells for Farrow."

"Real nice, Beebo. You sure do know how to find them, don't you?"

"I find on the beach after water come. I learn all shell an' find all on the beach."

"How can you find them so easily, Beebo?"

"I see good." The old man squinted and pointed toward the ocean. "I see all the way to water. You see shell there?"

Hendrick looked and nodded his head. "Just barely, Beebo. Can you see far away too?"

"I see all the boats in the water. An' I see all up an' down sand."

Hendrick stood and looked inland. He could not see past the dunes but remembered that Stassen's test area lay further south. He knew that the dunes leveled out on down the island. Hendrick watched Beebo separate the bigger shells from the others, then casually, he picked up the largest one on the sand before him and held it for Beebo's inspection.

"You like these big ones, Beebo?"

Beebo smiled broadly, his apparent mistrust of Hendrick subsiding. "Beebo like big shell."

"Is this the biggest you've found?"

Beebo nodded and held out his hand. Hendrick gave him the shell. "I know where there are bigger ones, Beebo."

"Where you see?"

Hendrick pointed toward the south end of the beach. "Down there. I just saw them. Let's go down there, and I'll show you where they are."

The old man carefully placed the big shells in his pocket and the rest in the paper sack. He stood and watched Hendrick who pointed again and nodded encouragingly. They walked toward the water's edge and down the beach, stopping occasionally to pick up shells. Hendrick presented a shell and asked if Beebo thought it worth keeping. Some, he took from Hendrick and placed in the sack; others he hurled as far into the ocean as he could.

"What do you see when you are out here by yourself, Beebo?"

"I see the shells an' the water. After the water come in an' go away, it bring shell an' I pick up all the good shell."

"I know, Beebo." Hendrick glanced at his watch. One-twenty. "But what else? Do you ever see anybody on the beach or across there?" They had reached the open area near Stassen's test plot. When Beebo looked in that direction, his expression changed noticeably. He appeared nervous and more tense. His gaze shifted between the sandy beach and the ocean. As if struggling to decide what he should do, Beebo's body movements quickened. He jerked his head in different directions, looking for some imminent danger.

"Do you remember seeing Dr. Stassen over there, Beebo?"

"No! Don't want to talk Stassen."

"Why, Beebo? Did he hurt you or scare you?"

"Stassen evil. Don't want to talk."

"Now, take it easy, Beebo. Nobody's going to hurt you. Where did you see Stassen? How do you know he was evil?"

"Jaheewah get him. Jaheewah take evil off island. Jaheewah don't like talk about bad people. I see Jaheewah get Stassen."

"You saw him? Where, Beebo? Show me."

The old black man pointed toward the estuary where Stassen had last been seen, then with a quick gesture of his hand, signaled to Hendrick for silence. Beebo had heard the drone of the light plane before Hendrick and before either could see it. Beebo began a pitiful, frightened moan that increased in pitch and intensity with the approach of the plane. Hendrick had heard nothing like it. In a few seconds, the plane appeared over the trees lining the beach to the north and tightly banked for a run down the water's edge. Hendrick watched Beebo, trying desperately to imagine what the superstitious and frightened old man saw. The plane quickly descended and sped directly, menacingly, at the two men. Hendrick, somewhat unnerved himself, grabbed Beebo's arm, attempting to control him. The plane bore down on them, its roaring engine shattering the hot stillness of the afternoon. Beebo began to scream in short guttural gasps as if being bludgeoned with a club, yelling over and over: "Jaheewah! Don't get me! DON'T GET ME! Noooo. . ."

Just before the plane passed over them, a hissing spray spewed out of the tanks mounted under the wings.

"*Jaheewah*," Beebo screamed "*Jaheewah!*" He pushed Hendrick away and bolted up the beach away from the fumes and the departing plane.

"Beebo! Beebo! Wait!" Hendrick yelled and chased after the terrified man. He quickly closed the gap between them, but Beebo turned and plunged into the thick underbrush of the woods. Hendrick had just caught Beebo's arm when a tree branch swung back hitting, the side of his head. The sharp pointed leaves of young saw palmetto turned into green daggers stabbing up at him, and above him, tall pine trees began to spin. Then . . . he was unconscious.

Hendrick came to slowly, aware of only a blinding shaft of sunlight and the uncomfortable position his body had assumed when he fell. A mosquito, the largest he had ever seen, quietly busied itself relieving Hendrick of a few milliliters of blood. Hendrick struck viciously at the insect, smearing his own blood over his arm. His attempt to stand brought with it the painful awareness of his head injury. He slowly rose to his feet and dizzily returned to the beach. *"Good lord,"* he muttered to himself, *"There's no telling where the hell Beebo is now."*

Hendrick's head ached, and he had bled enough to make his injury appear more serious than it actually was. What to do? He had to find Beebo and knew he would need help. He ran back to the Institute and burst into Farrow's office, out of breath with the side of his head covered with dried blood.

"Mr. Hendrick! What on *earth* happened to you?"

"A tree limb just about took my head off, Jackie. Where's Dr. Farrow?"

"Just a minute ago he called up from the dock. They're down there looking over some damage to one of the boats. Is there anything I can do?"

"Yeah. Get him on the phone, if you can—right away."

Jackie quickly dialed three digits and then spoke excitedly. "Who is this? Jason? Is Dr. Farrow still there?" She nodded to Hendrick. "Mr. Hendrick wants to talk to him."

"Farrow."

"This is Hendrick. I've got a problem."

"So have I, Bob. But what can I do for you?"

"It's Beebo. He's run away, and he's hysterical."

"*What*? You'd better explain that, Mr. Hendrick."

"We were on the beach—down at the south end. He and I were talking about Stassen, and a plane flew over us and scared him. He took off running up the beach, and just before I caught him, a tree branch knocked me unconscious. When I came to, he was nowhere to be seen." Hendrick noticed the clock on the wall. "He's been gone at least an hour."

"A plane? What in the hell was a plane doing over here?"

"I ordered it."

"*You* ordered it?"

"I needed to see how Beebo would react.

255

"Why you stupid bastard! You *knew* he was afraid of planes. Why in the hell would you do a goddamn thing like that?"

"We can talk about it later. What about Beebo?"

Hendrick heard Farrow barking orders to Jason.

Mr. Hendrick, we'll all meet at the maintenance barn in fifteen minutes. I assume since you're responsible for this, you wouldn't mind helping us find him?

"I'll be there."

"Good." Farrow hung up with no other comment.

"Jackie, is there a restroom where I might clean up?"

She had already taken the first aid kit from a closet and filled a small bowl with warm water. "Just sit down here, Mr. Hendrick. I can take care of that cut for you."

His head bandaged and clean, Hendrick thanked her and went immediately to the maintenance area where several of the maintenance crew and some of the students had gathered. Their glares as Hendrick approached made it clear that they all knew Beebo's disappearance lay strictly on Hendrick's shoulders. The arrival of the jeep with Jason and Farrow inside curtailed any further conversation, and Farrow spoke first.

"Now, Mr. Hendrick, how far down the south beach were you when Beebo got away?"

"I lost him right at the edge of the dunes and just into the woods."

"And he ran on into the woods—toward the paved road?'

"Yes. And then I got hit and passed out."

Farrow turned to the circle of men. "Was anybody working down there this afternoon?" Three hands shot up. "Did you see Beebo cross the road?" The three men looked at one another and shook their heads.

"No sir. He didn't cross the road, or we would have seen him."

"Okay, Farrow continued. We may get lucky. That means he's in the woods between the road and the beach and not in the marshes like last time. We've got four or five hours of daylight, so let's get on it. You young people, if you haven't been in the woods before, keep your eyes peeled for snakes—rattlesnakes, copperheads, and water moccasins. This is a good time of day for them to be looking for frogs and lizards. Jason, Bill can take the truck, and we'll take the jeep. Bill, you'd better throw in one of the mattresses in case he's hurt. When we get down there, I want a line of people with about twenty yards between each of you. There's no point in calling to him, because he'll either not answer or worse, keep on running. So, just find him, and call out when you do. Oh, Bill . . . have one of the students call Dr. Palliston's office and tell him what's happening and to expect us as soon as we can find Beebo and get him back to the infirmary."

The men hurriedly climbed into the truck bed, and Farrow, Hendrick, and Jason took the jeep. The two vehicles sped down the main road until they reached the last turn-off leading through the woods to the beach. Farrow looked behind him, then signaled to stop.

"Hold it here a minute, Jason. Now, Mr. Hendrick, this is the last road going out to the beach. Do you remember if Beebo went into the woods below where this comes out?"

"I'm sure he did. We probably weren't more than a half-mile below the road when we were talking."

"All right. Jason, go back there, and tell them I want six or seven men within sight of each other working the area from the dirt road south through the woods. The rest of us will cover the area from the paved road on out to the beach. And tell Bill he can start dropping men off about every twenty-five yards or so until we run out of men or woods."

Jason relayed Farrow's instructions and returned quickly. In a few moments, the two lines were set, and Farrow waved for the sweep to begin. They had only gone a few yards when Hendrick began to realize the distinct possibility of not finding Beebo alive. Dense underbrush provided a lush environment in which thrived more insects, reptiles, and birds than Hendrick could fathom. The men steadily trampled through the woods, ignoring swarming pests and occasional snakes and lizards.

Nearly an hour had passed, and there was still no sign of the old man. Farrow signaled the search party to stop for a moment. Only about an acre of woods remained, and the line had tightened up, leaving only a few feet separating the searchers.

"Let's rest just a second—everybody quiet!" Farrow commanded. "I want to listen."

In seconds, the normal sounds of the woods returned. Hendrick watched exotic birds fly into the area and listened as their calls punctuated the humming and buzzing of insects. A quick rustling of leaves, and a marsh rabbit darted away from the waiting men. Farrow gave the signal to renew the search, when Jason raised his hand for silence.

"Wait . . . listen!" Jason whispered.

The line of men stood perfectly still, looking at Jason and Farrow, then into the woods. Hendrick heard nothing unusual, but Jason and Farrow nodded in silent agreement. Beebo was nearby. The tired men crept ahead. Soon, everyone could hear a soft moaning, whimpering cry, guiding the men to one of the large live oaks just a few hundred feet away. They trudged more carefully, more quietly, trying not to scare the panicked Beebo. The faint sound grew louder and more sustained. They slowly approached the base of the huge tree, not wanting to startle the old man further. Beebo lay huddled in the gnarled, exposed roots of the tree—wide-eyed, but catatonically oblivious to their presence. He lay trembling on his side, and the bleeding knuckles of two fingers were crammed into his slobbering mouth. His eyes were unfocused, glazed and terror-filled. His gray beard glistened with saliva and blood from his bitten fingers. Mosquitoes and sand gnats crawled across his face. Hendrick felt the reproving eyes of the men, and he sadly remembered his last words to Margaret Courtney: *"I'll look out for him."*

Farrow leaned down and slowly placed a hand on Beebo's shoulder.

"Easy, Beebo. You're okay. Take it easy, now. We're going to get you home. Okay Jason, let's get him out to the truck as easy as you can and take him straight to Dr. Palliston." He turned to Hendrick. "You stupid, meddling sonofabitch."

The men gently picked up the shivering Beebo and slowly headed for the truck. Farrow's words to Hendrick were the last anyone spoke until they reached the infirmary where Palliston stood waiting at the door. He had prepared a bed in a room off the main area but motioned the men to put Beebo on a nearby examining table. "I want him stripped and bathed after this injection. Who can help?" Jason, who was nearest Palliston, began to unpin Beebo's jacket. "Was he this calm when you found him?"

Farrow responded, "Not at all—he was trembling and salivating heavily. He's bitten his fingers, but I didn't see

261

any other wounds. What do you think, Palliston? He'll come out of this, won't he?"

"It's too soon to tell. I've sedated him pretty heavily, so he should sleep tonight and most of tomorrow. Then we'll see. If we're lucky, he might just wake up and think it was all a bad dream. What in the hell happened, anyway?"

Hendrick started to speak but Farrow cut him off. "I'll tell you later. Okay men. Beebo's going to be pretty much out of it but all right for tonight. You can all go on now and get cleaned up. Thank you very much for a good job. I appreciate your help. Oh, Jason? After supper, get a case or two of beer out of the cooler and take it down to the maintenance barn for the men. Tell them again how much I appreciate their help."

Jason left the office and followed the other men who slowly headed toward the dining hall.

"Dr. Palliston, may Mr. Hendrick and I use your office for just a moment or two?" Palliston had already begun his examination of Beebo but nodded. Hendrick entered the office, and Farrow shut the door behind them.

His face reddened with anger, Farrow exploded. "Mr. Hendrick, I am mad as hell at you. I don't know what you're trying to do. Since the day you came on this island to do a simple public relations job, you have nosed around as if there's some conspiracy, practically accused me of harboring a murderer, broken into one of our cottages, arranged for an airplane with no authority, and, if that's not enough, practically killed Beebo! Now before I call your editor and complain, I'd like to hear from you some goddam good rationale for your actions. And if I don't, I'm going to kick your ass off this island and seriously consider bringing assault charges on Beebo's behalf against you."

Hendrick's response to Farrow was immediate and in no way apologetic. He stared unflinchingly at Farrow and answered. "Now you listen to me, you pompous bastard. I haven't said anything all afternoon. You've had your fun embarrassing me in front of the others, and I didn't argue with you because I do feel badly about Beebo. But I have *had* it with your authority and your manipulation of me and everyone else. They may have to take it, but I sure as hell don't. You can blame me all you like for Beebo's situation, but, goddammit, it's just as much your fault as mine. If you had leveled with me about Stassen from the beginning, I probably would not have subjected Beebo to this. From the day I got here, you've played cat and mouse games with me and appointed Jason to watch my every move."

"I explained that!"

"Explained it, hell. You're running scared, Farrow and I'm going to lay it out for you. Because I know why. It was hard to figure, but, damn it, now I know. And after I get through, if you still want to call my editor, then that's just fine with me. I'm sure he will be interested in the murder of an internationally known scientist."

"Don't try to fast talk your way out of responsibility for your actions with wild accusations, Hendrick."

"All due respect, Dr. Farrow . . . just shut up and listen. We'll see how wild you think they are. In the first place, the coroner's report clearly shows that Stassen did *not* drown, and there is enough circumstantial evidence that he died from asphyxiation. He was an acute asthmatic, and his system would not tolerate any fumes from the insecticide you spray around here. Even your own secretary knew that Stassen was mortally afraid of the spray, and Palliston will confirm what it would do to him."

"Our trucks don't go down there."

"Come on, Farrow. I'm not stupid. A plane could not only reach him—it would be on him before he knew what was happening. I've confirmed that, don't you see. It's a damn clever way to kill somebody and not even be there. You knew he was down there, and you ordered the spraying of the area knowing that, as an asthmatic, he wouldn't survive. And if Beebo comes around, I've got an eyewitness, Farrow. Of course, he thinks it was Jaheewah, but it would be clear when explained to a court that, for Beebo, Jaheewah and an airplane are one and the same. He saw Stassen die—Beebo said so this afternoon."

"That's all very intriguing, but it's also clearly explained as an accident. You can't prove that I knew Stassen would be at the test plot when the area was to be sprayed. You're right. I did order the estuary sprayed, but I ordered it for a damn good reason and a week before it was done. That's all in our phone log. I couldn't have known Stassen would be there, and I didn't arrange for him to be at the site. I don't really care what you think of me, Hendrick, but do you actually regard me as the murderer? What possible motive would I have?"

"A motive? I admit I don't know exactly why just yet. But you've done some very suspicious things. Like, transferring Margaret out of Stassen's lab station and discontinuing all of Stassen's experiments almost immediately after his death. Furthermore, you've either destroyed or hidden Stassen's lab notebook. As far as I can tell, that would be the only written record of his main work here—there's nothing else in the files. You told me that the two of you weren't close, but you failed to mention the heated argument that Margaret overheard. Stassen feared for his life. I know that because of the two letters I found in his papers." For the first time, Farrow's expression betrayed a hint of apprehension. Hendrick wryly smiled. "You overlooked them, didn't you? Well, they're interesting, and in them, he says he has argued with you and was concerned about his safety." This was Hendrick's first lie, but he gambled that Farrow had indeed overlooked the letters. He pulled one from his pocket. "I have one here, and the other is put away." Hendrick paused to let that sink in, and neither of them spoke for awhile. Farrow's anger had diminished, and he seemed more introspective than irate. Farrow rested against the edge of the desk. Hendrick found the lack of conversation almost disarming—almost as if he had accused Farrow of a slight oversight, received an apology, and the whole matter was resolved.

"Okay, Hendrick. You've made your point, and although I honestly regret your suspicions of me and my motives, I don't blame you for having them. I admit you've been very thorough in your efforts, and you can probably make a reasonable case against me. And you can pursue it if you like—there's the phone. But I'm telling you quite candidly, you don't know half as much as you think you do. There are gaping holes in your conjecture, and you might like to know that there are others involved."

"Who?"

"Come on, Hendrick. Give me some credit. It depends on what you decide to do whether I tell you that or not. If you're content that I've murdered Stassen and that you have enough evidence to prove it, then you don't really need anything else from me—and by God, you won't get it. But if you pride yourself on being a first-class reporter and want to know what has happened here, then you must give me until later this evening to set up a meeting with everybody involved."

"You're stalling, Farrow."

"You're wrong. Think about it. The ferry's shut down for the day; I'm not about to take a boat out after dark, and we can't afford a helicopter. Where in the hell am I going? If I were you, I would trust me."

"Okay, Dr. Farrow. You've got your meeting. When and where?"

"Nine o'clock at my cottage."

Who'll be there?"

"Listen, Hendrick. You don't trust me. Why should I trust you? I won't have you harassing any of these people before tonight. Then, you can ask whatever you like. They'll be there."

"All right. But I'm leaving the island tomorrow morning with or without your explanation, and that's a promise."

"Fair enough. I want to talk to Palliston about Beebo. Then I have to set up the meeting. You'll excuse me?"

"Okay. I need to get cleaned up, but I'll be at your cottage at nine o'clock."

After seeing Beebo calmly sleeping, Hendrick walked to the barracks to take a quick shower and to meet Margaret. Afraid he had mentioned her too many times, he wanted her to be prepared should she have to face Farrow alone. And he owed her an explanation about Beebo.

By the time Hendrick met Margaret, it was dusk and was raining. The aroma of wet pine trees filled the air. As they sat alone on the porch bannister, he detailed to her the situation with Beebo, and she took it reasonably well— at least she seemed to understand the risk Hendrick had assumed. When he told her of his conversation with Farrow, she became less pensive and more concerned.

"Bob, you will be careful?"

"Of course. I don't really expect any fireworks. Besides, Farrow's admission that there is more than he's telling and that other people are involved is too intriguing to ignore. Oddly enough, I feel like today was the first honest talk I've had with him."

"Well . . . I'll wait here for you, but I want to know what's going on."

"Okay. I'll be back as soon as I can." Hendrick stood to leave. Margaret rose from the bannister and took his hand.

"Bob?"

"Yeah?"

"Please be careful."

"I will. I've got to go." Pulling his jacket tighter around his neck, he stepped off the porch toward Farrow's cottage.

JAHEEWAH

CHAPTER 13

Hendrick approached the H.I.'s cottage with not so much fear as curiosity. Farrow's call for a meeting at least implied a possible conspiracy against Stassen. What had Stassen done—what possible conflict existed that gave impetus for his murder?

At the door, Farrow politely greeted Hendrick and invited him into the living room where three other men sat waiting. Hendrick immediately recognized them as the senior staff of the Institute, two of whom, Frederick Gruber and Jack Morrison, he had spoken to briefly on the boat the day he arrived on the island. Acknowledging Hendrick's presence, the three men stood, then sat again on the couch. Millie had placed a pot of coffee and mugs on the coffee table and then was excused for the night. Farrow motioned Hendrick to the chair adjacent to the couch then took a seat across from Hendrick. He began the conversation in a quiet but authoritative manner.

"Mr. Hendrick, there are a few things I want to say before we discuss the reason we're here. I've asked Dr. Gruber, Dr. Morrison, and Dr. Holtzman to come only to better explain what I alone am responsible for. I indicated to you a certain involvement on their part, but I want to make clear that their involvement is—was only supportive in nature."

"I understand."

From a cardboard box beside his chair, Farrow withdrew a thick black notebook held shut by a wide rubber band. He handed it to Hendrick.

"I think this is what you've been most interested in. It's Dr. Stassen's lab notebook—a record of his experiments. I think you'll find the most recent entries quite disturbing."

Hendrick thumbed through the notebook. Margaret had not exaggerated. Every entry was logged by date and time—down to the minute. Though Stassen had printed terminology and procedures, comments in script concerning results or hypotheses unmistakably matched the note Margaret had found. To Hendrick, however, references to

272

chemicals, reactions, and procedures were beyond his comprehension.

"Perhaps, Dr. Farrow, it would simplify things if you just told me what in here made you feel you should remove it from Stassen's personal effects."

"Then you do recognize the notebook as Stassen's writings?"

"Yes."

"Well, we thought a series of experiments he began over a year ago would be productive and very beneficial in terms of toxicity control in the wetlands. As far as we knew, he was the only one inducing shrimp and other invertebrates to ingest chemically altered plankton to achieve a significant level of resistance to toxic substances. Dr. Stassen hoped, as did we all, that certain toxins from plants or oil spills would trigger a resistance in these adapted invertebrates so that they could slough off the poisons. After his death and after I had time to thoroughly study his notes, it became frighteningly clear that what I accused him of, and what he admitted to, was true. Jack? Would you like to continue?"

Morrison leaned forward to show Hendrick a portion of the notebook.

"Apparently, a year or so ago, if these dates are accurate, Dr. Stassen began a process of experimenting with increased amounts of carbon dioxide together with fertilizer. This would still allow photosynthesis to occur as well as dramatically increase the nutrient value of the phytoplankton. He told us he had two objectives: to improve the quality and increase the population of shrimp, and possibly, as Dr. Farrow said, to create some sort of immunity or at least a resistance to poisons in the estuarine areas."

"By simply dumping fertilizer in the water?"

"Basically, yes. Coastal areas don't normally have a high amount of nitrogen which the fertilizer provides. You see, the shrimp are 'consumers' in the food chain and are dependent upon the 'producers,' the plankton. Stassen had discovered that the fertilizer, soluble in saline water, catalyzes the ability of plant life—the plankton—to convert carbon dioxide to dissolved oxygen. It also provides a kind of transparent 'blanket' to hold the oxygen in the water. The shrimp would benefit from the highly oxygenated

274

water, and the plankton would become, in turn, more profuse and nutrient-laden for the shrimp to ingest."

"Which would make bigger shrimp?"

"Exactly. And healthier looking. Also, a substantial acceleration in their reproductive cycle would occur. The implications of increased reproduction alone are significant for the shrimping industry. It could almost triple the production."

Gruber added, "And that could mean a lot of money from shrimp companies for the process—which is why Stassen had learned of Allied Industries and their interest in his notebook."

Farrow's expression and nod revealed his knowledge of the possible transaction Allied Industries had proposed.

Morrison continued. "Perhaps. But we don't think Stassen had any concern about money. What did concern us is a particular ramification of Stassen's experiments which he left undisclosed and which are considerably more complex. Let me show you." Morrison pointed to a later section of the notebook. "If you'll notice, he began referring to something, we weren't sure what, as some sort of unnamed byproduct of the process, which he only identified with the initials 'H4N1.' Towards the last of the notes, he enters frequently: 'H4N1', established and confirmed'."

"You don't know what that is?"

"We didn't. But we do now. It's a combination of hemagglutinin and neuraminidase, both of which are glycoproteins."

"I have no clue what that means."

Morrison glanced at Farrow, who nodded, then looked back at Hendrick. "It's a genetically modified virus, Mr. Hendrick, an unknown virus, the virulence of which is unmeasured and limitless. The virus will attach to a healthy plankton cell and inject its genetic material into the host. Also, its transmission vectors include other organisms, and, ultimately, humans."

"You don't know anything about it?"

"We only know that once shrimp ingest the chemically altered plankton, the shrimp become healthy, active carriers of this virus. They're loaded with it. They spread the virus by reproductive spawning, and even their excrement can infect whatever ingests it. They can even brush

276

against a piling and transfer the virus to other organisms that come in contact with the piling. We're not sure, but we think even inanimate objects, like ships, coming in contact with these organisms, could also become fomites, and transport the virus to other locales—even worldwide."

"Could that affect a human? Can *humans* contract the virus by simply touching infected shrimp?"

"Again, we're not quite sure. But we do know that for some people to eat the infected shrimp is fatal—possibly within just a few hours."

"How do you know this?"

"Stassen made reference to tests of the virus in a human. We've concluded that Lawanda Moser was that unwitting index case. We reviewed Dr. Palliston's report on her presentation and his treatment, and the result is consistent with Stassen's speculation. The virus can lead to anemic disorder like sickle cell anemia or hemolytic anemia, but is catalyzed by corticosteroids sometimes prescribed to treat the anemia. In this case, the normal treatment constitutes a death sentence because you are fighting a virus and not the anemia. And it's a hell of a way to die. The virus penetrates the central nervous sys-

277

tem resulting in immediate loss of muscular control. The muscles themselves contract violently, causing excruciating pain. Within a period of one to three hours, blood pressure builds up above 300 over 160 causing multiple aneurisms and imminent death."

Hendrick asked, "But why would only she die?"

"Ironically, the virus can only thrive and attack anyone who is Rh- negative."

"But doesn't there have to be at least one other Rh-negative person in the family—I assume the mother, since the father, presumably as well as the rest of the family, ate the shrimp and were unaffected?"

Farrow answered. "That confused us too until I remembered that Moser had remarried after his first wife had died, and Lawanda was from that marriage. Dr. Palliston's records show her mother to be Rh-negative and the rest of the family Rh-positive. Stassen had an ideal test situation to prove that results would be terminal to only Rh-negative subjects. Obviously, he was correct."

"But what you're suggesting is murder of people who happened to be Rh-negative. You're telling me Stassen would really *do* that?"

Farrow continued, "Well, Mr. Hendrick, I must now tell you some things that I had decided not to share earlier. We feel that Dr. Stassen did not consider himself a murderer. We think he simply became consumed by an overwhelming need for revenge. His wife and baby and other relatives were living in Dresden during World War II. Dresden suffered terribly. The Allies bombed it nearly into oblivion. Tens of thousands died—and maybe, unnecessarily—including all of Stassen's family. In some of his letters, he writes about their survival of one of the first bombing raids and his decision to stay away from home to complete some marine studies. He assumed that the Allies wouldn't bomb the same city again. He was wrong. Dresden sustained four or five more raids but his family and relatives did not survive. In one of his letters, he expresses extreme guilt about his decision not to return to Dresden. He repeats several times that, had he been there, he could have gotten them all out into the countryside or at least died with them. I've kept his last letter to his wife. She had been dead for some time, but he still wrote letters to her but, of course, never mailed them. I've kept this one in case we were ever questioned about all of this. I don't know if you read German, but Dr. Gruber can translate if you like."

Hendrick took the letter from Farrow, comparing it with the others he had seen, then handed it to Gruber. "Please."

Gruber began, "It is dated approximately a month before he died. As Dr. Farrow says, he continued to write to her as though she were still alive.

mein Geliebte:

I kiss the sweet memory of your beautiful face from the terrible solitude you left me. This will be my last letter for a while—my long-awaited project is nearly completed, and I must soon prepare for my departure. As it is only your understanding and forgiveness that are important to me, I confess the following to you only.

It is so difficult for me to describe what has become terribly complex and now irrevocable but somehow I feel it necessary to tell you everything that has happened and that will happen. When they took you and Angelika from me, I vowed vengeance and a visitation of our suffering on even those as innocent as you and our loved ones. At that time, I had no knowledge of how this could be accomplished, but I knew it would be through my work.

280

In my most recent letters, you may have guessed that I was very near the solution. I did not want to tell you more until I was absolutely certain of its implementation and result.

And now, I am certain. It is alarmingly simple. I have introduced fertilizer into the shrimp tanks, which affects the plankton. I then created a modified virus that attaches to the plankton. The shrimp ingest the plankton and grow healthier in every respect, with the exception that introduced in their system is the virus, the lethality of which is almost unbelievable. I have tested it on a girl with the result that logical drug treatments exponentially compound the deadliness of the virus. I have determined to my satisfaction that there is no antiviral treatment and once contaminated material is eaten, death is imminent. I have treated the estuary. Now, it is only a matter of time.

My darling, I must tell you that I feel like the lemming that supposedly races to the sea. I, too, proceed resolutely to my own demise. At those who think they control their own destiny, I simply laugh, for though my heart and mind tell me what I am vengefully doing is inhumane and wrong, I no longer have the strength or the will to stop the process. But . . . I am only the pilot—not the bomb. Somehow in all this I cannot consider myself a murderer, for a murderer, an assassin, knows his victim. I have no concern at all for the victims. It is not important who must die, but how. They must be innocent, anonymous, and unprotected. Was it not the same for you—for our loved ones?

I realize, my dearest, you will condemn my actions and beg me to stop, but ultimately, this will bring us together. Now that it is begun, I am strangely reconciled to its end. Whether it is completed or not, I leave to fate both judgement and resolution.

I reach for the both of you in the darkness, my darlings, and convince myself that you are there. Kiss our beautiful Angelika for me a thousand times, as I kiss you in my loneliness.

Mit all meiner Liebe, Heinrich

"You see, Mr. Hendrick," Gruber continued, "Except for this misguided plan of his, Dr. Stassen was a brilliant scientist, albeit somewhat eccentric. But nonetheless, Stassen set in motion a monster of destruction as lethal as any bomb. We are talking about infecting shrimp all along the entire Eastern Seaboard, and just one foreign ship

282

leaving a viral deposit on a piling helps transport the virus to other ships and other destinations. Once the virus is established, with no known antiviral treatment, there would be a massive outbreak and the deaths of hundreds of thousands of innocent people."

Hendrick shook his head. "That's what I can't understand about you people. How in God's name can you sit on this?"

Farrow calmly reached for a mug, poured himself more coffee, and motioned to the others who declined.

"Mr. Hendrick, let me try to explain the dilemma facing me as Head of the Institute and perhaps some justification for my inaction—fully aware that there are sins of omission as well as commission. Stassen, his reputation and credentials, intimidated many of us here. I gave him as wide a berth as I could so as not to hamper his work. What he has done for marine biology, specifically in poisoning control, is immeasurable. To reveal this monstrous plan of his is to negate the validity of his recent work and invalidate his reputation and the contributions he has made. Selfishly, I also realized it would certainly mean the end of the Institute. However, I am not as callous or inhumane as you seem to think. I did confront him with

283

what I suspected, and I threatened him with expulsion and exposure to the authorities. At first, he was irate but did not deny anything. Afterwards, he became rather unconcerned with my accusations. He calmly informed me that he would soon find a way to continue. In short, only his death could stop him. When I checked the chemical supplies against invoices, I felt sure he must have already contaminated the estuary. Now, Mr. Hendrick, I know you have me pegged as a murderer, but I assure you, I didn't know *what* to do about Stassen. My first concern—my objective—was to somehow stop the process. Later, I would have to deal with Stassen. I knew we were in trouble, but I also knew that we were in a better position to deal with the problem than anyone else in the world. The four of us here knew exactly what Stassen had been working on and figured out roughly when he had treated the area. We considered trapping or killing all of the shrimp. The threat would have been neutralized. In searching for some way to do that, I remembered a time Stassen came to me insisting that I fire one of the maintenance staff. Stassen had found all of the shrimp in the test tanks dead one morning. In cleaning up and spraying for mosquitoes and insects, the worker had inadvertently gotten spray into the tanks. We were puzzled as to why that would kill the shrimp, but apparently Stassen realized that the spray had reacted with the chemical he was using and killed the shrimp. I thought we could try the same thing. It was a gamble but one I thought we should take. I called the air service and asked them to saturate the test area with mosquito repellent. Next, we planned to close off the channel leading into the estuary with fine nets and wait. I ordered the spraying for mid-morning at low tide so that the process could begin with the tide coming in rather than out. Then, after several hours, we would gather the dead shrimp as well as the plankton and burn them."

"How did you get Stassen out there to get rid of him? You don't deny knowing that the spray would kill him as well?"

"I called him that morning to tell him that he was through, that I had ordered the area sprayed. But I couldn't get him on the phone. One of the students told me he had just taken Stassen out to the estuary in the motorboat. Hell yes, I knew what would happen if I didn't get him out of there, but I began to think about what he had already done to the Moser girl and the fact that he said he would not rest until he had carried out this horrible plan. You can call it murder if you like, but he set up the process by introducing the chemical, he had already acted

285

to commit murder thousands of times over, even if we were able to stop him. If somehow he escaped the spray . . . okay. But I could not let myself help him out of it."

"And you didn't alert the company to abort the spraying?"

"That's right. And although I take full responsibility, my colleagues have endorsed my actions by their silence—which was not required of them."

"And you became the judge."

"I guess so, Mr. Hendrick. And while I take no pleasure in the decision, no pleasure in Stassen's death, and regret the loss of his mind to the scientific community, I certainly do not regret that we have stopped him."

"What if you haven't?"

"We are confident we have. The day after the spraying, we dammed the estuary and waited. In just a few hours, every living organism—all the phytoplankton and zooplankton—was destroyed. The dead shrimp settled on the surface. We gathered all the hazardous material and burned it. We feel certain that the threat is over because it didn't appear that the spawning had occurred."

"You still haven't convinced me you should keep this information to yourself. Isn't it possible that some of the infected shrimp could have survived?"

"Yes, I suppose; but we don't think so. But look, Mr. Hendrick. Let's say we alert first the scientific community. It would have to be worldwide because of shipping routes. Your friends in the press would have a field day. The news would knock the bottom out of the shrimp industry. Now, this doesn't concern me as much as scaring the hell out of everyone who eats shrimp—scaring them unnecessarily if we have been successful in stopping the growth and spread of the virus. Okay, we destroy the shrimp market then say 'actually, there's nothing to be alarmed about.' How many people would ignore an accurate warning after that? Just think about the cancer scares and, for example, mass flu inoculations. Public trust is not what it ought to be and probably with good reason. We made a decision, Mr. Hendrick, and we think it's best to keep this between us and on the island. Now, I tried to keep you out of this, but you persisted. So, now you have a decision to make. You are free to do what you feel you must, but I urge you to think it through. You now know as much as we do, and consequently, you are now a part of the problem as much as we."

Farrow fell silent, and the tension grew. Hendrick busily and quietly considered all that he had heard and what had now become solely his decision. He felt convinced that Farrow would do no more to stop him and equally certain that his life was in no danger. Farrow had not only gambled on control of the estuary but now gambled on Hendrick—on his sense of right and wrong. Also, the odds were bad, for Hendrick himself could not formulate a clearly tenable position. Early on, he had maintained the opinion that manslaughter or even justifiable homicide is still homicide and should be punishable regardless. No one has the right to cause the death of another, and people have a moral obligation to intervene if it will prevent a death. Yet, Stassen's murder confused Hendrick because Stassen himself would have become the most heinous of murderers.

Hendrick broke the long silence.

"Is there anything else?"

Farrow responded, "No, that's it."

"Well, I've got to sort all this out. I can't give you any decision now—maybe in the morning before I leave we'll talk again, Dr. Farrow."

"Alright, Mr. Hendrick. I'll be available."

Hendrick stood, as did the others, and left. As expected, Margaret Courtney sat waiting for him on the barracks porch.

"Bob, I was beginning to worry."

"Yeah, I figured. But I had to hear them out."

"Them? Who was there?"

"Farrow and three senior residents."

"What happened? What's it all about?"

"It's very involved, and right now, I don't know how I feel—what I should do."

They sat talking in the darkness, and Hendrick related the entire discussion.

Margaret knew too much for him to try to protect her, and he felt she deserved to know everything. As he told her of Stassen's letter, he thought she began to cry. He took her hand, and after a while, they just sat together and didn't talk.

Finally, Hendrick stood. "I'm leaving tomorrow, Margaret, regardless of what I decide to do."

"I know."

"I'll see you before I go. Breakfast?"

"Okay." She stood and wrapped her arms around Hendrick's neck. He held her as she continued. "Bob, I feel very sad for Stassen. I liked him despite his gruff aloofness, and it's a rotten way for him to end up."

"I know. It would be simpler if he were not so easily understood, and if I didn't believe Farrow. Yet, there's no way I can justify Stassen's actions, and I don't think I can allow Farrow the privilege of disposing of him in that way. No matter how you try to rationalize it, it's still murder, and whether it's by omission or commission makes little difference. I've just got to think about it for a while—a long while."

Margaret pulled back, looking at Hendrick in the darkness. He started to release her but, obeying an impulse, kissed her softly on her forehead, then covered her mouth with his. She responded, and he felt her move closer to him. They embraced for a long time before he spoke.

"I'm not sure I need this diversion. But I welcome it."

She smiled, "Goodnight, Bob. Thanks for that."

"Don't mention it. My pleasure."

"I'm serious."

"I know. You'd better go in. I've got to go for a walk and do some thinking." He kissed her again, then left her at the door and stepped off the porch. When he looked back, she had gone in.

Hendrick walked for nearly an hour, thinking and listening to the sounds of the night. By the time he got to his room, his leg muscles ached from the distance he had walked. But he had reached a decision. Tomorrow, Farrow would know, and Hendrick would take the boat to the mainland.

JAHEEWAH

CHAPTER

14

Hendrick awoke a little after daybreak and lay in his bunk for a long while. He had always liked this time between awakening and rising. In the city, the sounds of people beginning their day seemed to wash away problems of the night. Hendrick always found a shower and a fresh shirt in the morning invigorating—even symbolic. In the preceding few days, he had become anxious to leave the island. And now, faced with the realization that filing a single story could determine the fate of the Institute and affect hundreds of thousands of lives, he wished it all in the past. Except for Margaret. In her case, the future interested him. Hendrick felt certain she would no doubt stay on the island, at least, for the time being.

He had packed most of his things the previous night. After a long walk and a hot shower, he dressed and left his room for the dining hall. Entering the hall to an enticing aroma of coffee, homemade biscuits, sausage, bacon, and the thick, white gravy to which he had become addicted, Hendrick glanced at a corner table to see Margaret smiling at him over a cup of coffee she held carefully against her lips. She joined him to go through the line then sought a more secluded table. They talked about the future of the Institute and her work. As he thought, she had decided to stay. Neither of them feared any reprisals from Farrow.

"Will you go down to the dock to see me off?"

"No. I'd rather say goodbye here, Bob."

"I don't mean to say goodbye—just to see me off. I want you to come to the city when you leave here, or I'll come down to Hagers Point. I want to see you—I want to be with you more."

"Maybe I will. What about Farrow? Will you talk to him before you leave?"

"Yes."

"And?"

"I'm going to walk away from it, Margaret. I never thought I would ever do that, but that's exactly what I'm going to do. Perhaps Beebo is right. Stassen represented a pitiable but nonetheless evil force on the island, and, in a way, Jaheewah did remove that evil. I feel sorry for Stassen. But not nearly as sorry as I would feel watching people die the way they would have. Even though Farrow is guilty, I think he made the right decision. An eye for an eye, I guess."

Hendrick noticed Jason approaching the table.

"Mr. Hendricks . . . Miss Courtney," Jason interrupted.

"Oh, hello Jason."

"Mr. Hendricks, I just wanted to let you know that Farrow's down at the dock to see you on your way. I got the jeep ready to take you down there whenever you're ready."

"Right. My bags are just outside. I'll be with you in a minute. Well, Margaret. I'll see you. I'll call you when I get settled. And I mean that."

"I know. I'll write, okay?"

"Sure. Me too."

Hendrick stood, gave Margaret a brief hug, and walked to the jeep. The ride to the dock shook Hendrick's breakfast unmercifully, but he enjoyed the drive. He and Jason talked about the island, and before stepping out of the jeep, Hendrick thanked Jason for the ride and his help while on Jaheewah. Turning, Hendrick saw Farrow sitting alone on the bench at the edge of the dock and sat down next to him. Farrow seemed far away—staring, watching the water and the birds across the marsh grass which lined the inland waterway.

"Good morning, Mr. Hendrick. Slept well, I trust?"

"Yeah, I did."

"Good." The two men sat quietly, looking across the water toward the marshes of the mainland. Neither seemed uncomfortable with the silence. They could just as easily have been two old fishing buddies who were content to sit and listen to the ripples of the water lapping against the side of their boat.

After several minutes, Farrow interrupted the quietness. "You'll be pleased to know that I've received some interesting correspondence this morning. Last night, the legislature okayed a 25 percent increase in our funding and supported additional staff requests. Your articles were good, and I'm sure they helped. I appreciate that. Very much.

"Thanks, I'm glad."

The two men again grew silent and watched the ferry arrive and unload passengers and supplies. As a blast of the horn called passengers aboard, Farrow stood and offered his hand. "You may find this hard to believe, Mr. Hendrick, but I do appreciate knowing you. Whatever you decide about Stassen, I'm sure you will be doing what you think best."

"Thank you, Dr. Farrow. But as of right now, you won't be hearing from me regarding Stassen. As far as I'm concerned, this story belongs here on Jaheewah—and I don't. Goodbye, and thanks for your hospitality."

"You're welcome. And, just know, we would be happy to have you come back anytime. Have a safe trip."

Hendrick nodded, then stood to board the boat. Farrow waved to the captain, turned, and walked toward the jeep where Jason sat waiting.

The mid-morning sun burned brightly—slowly dissipating the usual morning mist. Hendrick sat alone outside the enclosed cabin with his thoughts. Looking first at the shoreline and then the churning wake of the boat's twin props, he sensed that someone—something—stared at him. He looked to confirm the fact that he was the only passenger outside. A loud screech from above grabbed his attention. The huge black bird gracefully soared along the path of the boat just twenty feet above its rigging, his gaze fixed upon Hendrick.

"Go on back," Hendrick said aloud. "I'm gone now. The island's all yours."

The bird screeched again. With a subtle twist of his outstretched wings, the bird caught the wind and raced back toward Jaheewah. Hendrick smiled, shook his head, and waited anxiously for the mainland dock to appear on the horizon.

One year later.

ATLANTA (AP). Medical officials in the Georgia seacoast town of Brighton have reported a series of unexplained deaths to the State Board of Health. Brighton's Dr. John McAaron, in an interview with the Atlanta Constitution, stated: "*What disturbs us is the similarity of these eighteen deaths and the fact that, as far as* _we can determine, the victims have nothing in com-mon other than living here. It has the hallmarks of some sort of infectious virus, but we have been unable to identify it._" State health officials indicate no cause for alarm but acknowledge that an epidemiologist from the Center For Disease Control has been sent to the area.

JAHEEWAH

61416242R00183

Made in the USA
Lexington, KY
09 March 2017